La Maga
An Inner Journey

CAROLA CASTILLO

La Maga
An Inner Journey

by Carola Castillo.

English Translation: Cristina Alvaradejo-Hughes
Proof Reading: Mariana Galdo

ISBN 978-1-943083-02-2
ISBN 978-1-943083-03-9 (ebook)

www.carolacastillo.com

To my grandmothers Celia & Cristina

To Anita, the woman who kept my mother alive.

The transmission of a means to grow from spirit
must be from heart to heart, from one
human being to another in word and energy;
a very personal religion.

Without a guide —or teacher—
there can be no relationship nor learning.

One must be in love
with the source to really know the
extent of one's passion.

La Maga

Table of Contents

Glossary

mage

n. Now arch. & literary. LME.
(Anglicized f. Magus. Cf. (O) Fr. mage)

1. A magician; a person of exceptional wisdom and learning. LME. 2 spec.= Magus I. LME

2. J. I. M. Stewart I might be in the presence of a mage or a wizard in disguise.

The New Shorter Oxford. English Dictionary. © Oxford University Press 1973, 1993, New York. p.1661

mage

n –s (ME, fr. L magus – more at Magic)

1. Magician

2. Magus

Webster's Third New International Dictionary of the English Language. The definitive Merriam-Webster Unabridged Dictionary of the English Language. © 1986.

maga *(Spanish; Castilian)*

A woman said to be a mage.

Dedication

To those who gave me life, and the source of magic.

Body, mind and spirit that are endowed with a name this time around.

To the older siblings—all of them—and, especially, to the ones that show me the legacy that is written in the stones.

To the Mages and the Older Teachers, especially to "you" and your infinite legacy, the one that taught me the path toward *La Maga*.

To the events that made me grow up to be able to capture them on this paper.

To the people who fought against me and made me surrender to the revelation of truth.

To Mother Earth, who nourished me during the storms of words.

To *Cognitio Books & Apps*, able to connect the invisible and follow the "signs," giving shape to reality so that everyone has access to what is visible.

To the travel companions, the authentic ones, that guided me during violent hours when we were sipping the cosmos.

To the men and women that loved me without knowing that I loved them.

To the artists that in their color palette thought that I would have a tonality.

To the children that carry on life and stories.

To the initiated that make magic possible.

Come into my world without fear;
I transform it into joy.
Let me lead you from disguised failure, to universal happiness.
I am, in essence, beyond opposing forces with the capacity to
awaken.
My world originates from the invisible so that you follow your heart.
Nature is my ally,
hence the origin of storms and winds.
I let my body rest next to my mind;
so I can be asleep and alert.
I am immortal, since the truth that is in you never dies until it is
safely revealed.

I am *La Maga*,
your Mage,
the one for whom you have searched
and who now finds you.
I can see all and always know all,
since I do not deceive myself.
Time does not exist;
everything is revealed without endings.

From the cosmos...

First Path

"The encounter"

When I arrived she was already sitting with her usual calmness. There was a silence so blessed that it allowed you to maneuver in uncharted directions, the manner or cause was not important. Always admired, magical woman of my days. Rosy sunset skin. A hidden and enigmatic moon.

We have talked many times in person; some others, by phone.

However, in this encounter, a more intimate one, I was faced with the danger of believing I was special. I knew that my issue was of always coming from a place of arrogance and pride, believing, all the time, that I was better than everyone else. This kept me invariably far away from reality and the constant flow of life. A certain stubbornness of not wanting to face life; its force constantly dragged me to places that left me exposed to do the necessary work in the presence of light.

As about to undertake a narrative, a legacy or a transmission of something that no one acquires *'just like that.'*

I was about to encounter a ray of life, full of soul and wisdom; something that, at the end of the story, would be crucial and necessary for you to grasp, as I did.

The Mage has been lost in the world of the mundane and the everyday, a woman that by simply gazing at her—or listening to her —makes your heart tremble. You know she possesses something that is not of this world; however, her simplicity transports you to distant places like life itself. Sharing this journey by her side has been a great gift. Being close to her, more than querying her, has changed the direction of my life, its quality and the way that I manage to anchor my feet on the ground these days.

"Indeed life exists." The Mage and her presence are like virtues that give you unknown strengths; she will reveal mysteries and enigmas to the extent that your shoes can walk the path.

She comes from that place—as she declares—that we all seek outside of ourselves.

The place that is waiting to be revisited and that is inside of each one of us, waiting to give us its treasures.

She works together amongst shamans, sages and powerful forces that she respects and is transported away by, knowing the risk involved.

Mother Earth is the cardinal point of her gaze, which is how she determines the direction of her path. This sphere of movement allowed me to share the space, to open my eyes to other paths. At times she revealed its essence, and remained for me in order to be able to receive it. She could see "the totality" while I pretended, from my sheltered place, to be perplexed.

Some days were very tempestuous in me. She knew by heart the flaws in my soul.

At first, interviewing her was like an assignment; inquiring, corralling, pursuing so as to take from her what I thought was important. However, between entry and exit doors, without suspecting that throughout the quest one can encounter ghosts that are waiting to be revisited, the course of the winds changed, spinning round the vessel of my soul, and, with no warning of dangerous currents, I ended up alone with myself on an island... as a dying castaway, hungry of soul and without my intrinsic distractions. I had to reinvent life—my life. I learned of the nights that guide you toward the light, the significance of the stars, and the knowledge of universal magic.

For a long time, I loved her as the greatest love on Earth; at other times, I hated her, knowing myself frustrated and faced with my own reality.

She, without changing you, changes you. Without touching you, she entangles you with unfamiliar words called 'love,' 'compassion,' and 'strength.' In the end and without alternatives, you feel only satisfaction, even with the harshness that she uses to awaken you.

I still have not been able to comprehend if what you are about to read is a story, a tale, or perhaps the beginning of an initiatory path. That is the effect that she has, nothing is ever as you think or might have believed.

Many times she had me wait in silence, so that I would decide what words were necessary to use.

From time to time she would only look at me, and would simply guide me into her turbulent waters saying: "What do you want from me?" A question that took me to an infinite, eternal abyss.

Now that I am within steps of starting my story, I feel that exhilaration and fear which appears in her presence. Perhaps I respect something which cannot be understood and which we all desperately seek. To attempt to reveal or pretend to portray her is complete chaos for anyone who hopes to second-guess or circumscribe her. Yet, I can accomplish such a thing when I make the attempt.

My advice is for you to flow with these words. They can have meaning in spaces that no one still can understand from within the mind.

Abandon yourself to the swell of the waves that the full moon celebrates without a reason. One has to be compassionate with a story that can be transformed into a therapeutic journey of life.

Hang on, be persistent, commit, do something with passion, smile every second of life. Become aware of where you come from, what you want and where you are going.

This is how this master, Mage of the universe, left me while each one of us could accidentally clash with the path already traced by the stars and the cosmos.

I dedicate this book to the many hours spent with her that now seem lifetimes ago. With neither space nor time, some place far away, a path in life. Wherever she is, she will be freely doing her own things to carry the magic that consecrates her to each place.

She is disguised as something earthly—from the usual place—confusing even the most astute who claims they could challenge the infinite love that she possesses. This leaves you with the greatest lesson.

If you receive signals in the shape of feathers, it's her. If you hear that the wind is able to speak, it's her. Just observe carefully, in the end all the signs will always be:

Her.

This account is to begin living in the alchemy of her extraordinary presence.

May Mother Earth be kind with the journey that you are about to undertake.

"The path is made by walking"

I am a journalist, teacher and psychologist, confessed lover of the ancient arts that work to aid and heal the heart.

Seeker of seekers. In those endeavors I met the Mage, on an ordinary day of the most important years to come.

How could I forget when I saw her for the first time in Germany; it was a jolt to my soul. Subsequently I embarked on the great crusade that, thereafter, was difficult to stop. I travelled to many cities, in and out of my internal and external boundaries. I liked it, it filled me up, it changed me. In due time, I wanted so much or even more that I started to design proposals to obtain something else from her. After some time she was able to identify me in the groups of the initiated; she greeted me cold and distant. It would break my heart when I heard her say to me, "You haven't done much and you're still here. Healing is action, don't forget it. Take action before it's too late."

I wanted to ask her a lot of questions and she would always finish by saying, "The search is directly proportional to the void that we create."

During some of the meetings, we would stumble into each other on the premises where the activities were taking place. She would look into my eyes and say, "Get out of the way."

"Find your heart. Be honest." At the end of her work, the only thing I could get from her was, "What do you want from me?" This is how I started to love her, because I didn't even know what I wanted from me. After those first encounters, my love for her opened up roads that were intent on being abandoned. The little girl didn't want to grow up, wounds obscured my horizons, and my irresponsibility toward myself led me to lift the veils that would soon change me.

Many times I was content simply watching and adoring her. How easy it was to stay in that comfort, and settle in...

I looked like a fool intoxicated by her presence; her voice; the way she moved her hands; her gestures; her sense of humor. She used irony to smack consciences. Often, after these demonstrations of intelligence and wisdom, I would barely say with a sigh, "God, what a creature!"

I had to turn her into my icon. My teacher, my guru and hero: All of these! Absolutely everything that you want to accomplish in an instant and that cannot be achieved, unless you decide to open up the fractures of the heart to let the light in.

The Mage would perform very powerful interventions. My favorite was, "The use of the shovel." When someone put up resistance, she would say with love and simplicity, "For tomorrow, I want you to bring a shovel to dig the ground, as I will show you how to dig your own hole. We'll make your funeral and burial. Then we'll know if you have been alive or playing with life."

The group's response and mine were almost immediate. Most astonishing was the seriousness of the person who had been assigned that monumental task. The Mage knew with whom, how and where to do this.

Finally, the day of the meeting that I had yearned and wished for arrived. Her next stop would be a small town in a beautiful place called Groningen, in Holland. In its period of greenery, in this spot on earth, the multitude of trees and its inhabitants are adornments that go back in time. The calmness and peaceful space of Groningen looks like a postcard when you arrive or bid farewell at its train station, where thousands of stories are safeguarded forever.

In this place, the Mage allowed me to fulfill my aspirations to see her again and to witness her power. In workdays of intense labour, day after day, we had the fortuity of a place close by where we could share a bite, coffee and candies, which were intended to fill up the recently discovered voids.

In a single breath, she managed to attack me without giving me a chance to shield myself.

I calmed my anxiety and searched for the serenity that didn't want to come forth. She looked at me straightforward with intense eyes. I felt she was inviting me to approach her. My legs were shaking, since I thought that her words would be exactly the same as before.

In a sweet voice she said: "Tomorrow afternoon, at the end of our session, I will wait for you at the back of this building."

I was petrified. With terror I replied, "*Maga*, all that is behind this place is an abandoned and very old cemetery."

Her gaze told me everything. She spoke with ice in her pupils, with a demeanor that got inside my bones and left me breathless. She warned me by saying, "Keep wrestling with yourself; you will understand it."

I lowered my head and surrendered once again before her power of cosmic perception.

My ignorance of the meaning of respect and wisdom continued to keep me on the fringe of life; I still doubted the word "faith."

I couldn't sleep that night. My head was spinning like an abandoned, rusty Ferris wheel, where children were once enthusiastic to be that high, very high. Where every turn was a chance to climb up, to realize and accomplish everything. The thrill in my stomach, along with the fear of the Ferris wheel, silenced all questions. I punished myself thinking of how lucky and unfortunate I was for interviewing her. I battered myself relentlessly with the sense that I would not know what the best questions would be. Granting me an encounter at a cemetery. Why there? Spinning and spinning around. The Ferris wheel — the fairground of my own life.

However my opinionated nature was still claiming victory in silence, rejoicing in its recently perpetrated conquest.

Within me, it would repeat a thousand times over, "In the end, with persistence, you will achieve what no one else was able to accomplish."

The dreams that we long for, aspire to and actualize out of struggle and confrontation, become paradoxical; this would be no exception.

I came to the meeting overwhelmed by intense apprehension, tender tears and tremors.

Agitated, I paced the area practicing my line that I had memorized tediously; "Good morning *Maga*, I am ready to undertake the biggest project that no one has ever proposed to you."

I repeated my line out loud again and again, without noticing how I was, little by little, eroding holes in the ground for me to fall into.

Long minutes started to pass, the remnants of the hourglass of my heart filled up the holes that opened at my feet.

The Mage was never late to any gathering. She honoured schedules and structures. However, for our meeting the pendulum struck and distressed me, emphasizing the heaviness of the time passed.

I was starting to get impatient and my memorized lines were crumbling in a situation where neither time nor word meant anything.

Hours… many thousands of minutes were my likely sentence, as I realized that she was not coming to the appointment. I was determined to think that maybe since this was a different event in her life, she would be taking the necessary time, or maybe she wanted me in this state of madness by making me wait…

Strange voices made themselves audible from within the moss of the guardian trees that attended the dead and their sacred land.

Fear took hold of me and I was about to give up.

Maga, Maga, come!

The sand in the hourglass continued passing, with a sound in my head that seemed more like a device about to explode in the midst of war.

I waited patiently and respectfully; she would know why she was leaving me to wait for such a long time.

I had to trust and remain.

I had already learned that arriving late to her activities was a way of saying that one *did not value* her teachings. Doing so repeatedly, the Mage would tell you without mercy, "You can leave the premises, anyone who is not kind and respectful with energy, should expect the same in return."

Each one of her sentences impressed me: "Anyone who is not kind and respectful with energy should expect the same in return." I would repeat it to myself a thousand times over.

In this way she showed me the imperceptible planes and left me knowing that heaven was here on Earth. Everything started here, in life. Later on, one could humbly reach heaven and its bliss.

It was logical and simple: the teacher always has something unexpected to teach or convey. To arrive late, would be to affirm that you did not value what was being transmitted to you. If you had a really good reason to do so, you were obliged to wait at the door, observe her with respect, wait for the moment when she made eye contact with you, then lower your head and enter in silence without disturbing the course of the teaching.

Later on, if she gave you the opportunity, you would give an explanation and offer your apologies. That was how her things worked. She knew that the most important lessons had to do with *respect*.

On the contrary, if she was the one that arrived late, we had to wait patiently, even for hours. If you think this was unfair, it's possible that you aren't mature enough for her great art. In this waiting, I learned so much … for this I'm also grateful to her.

Often times she arrived late to her lessons, and not by hours but by days. So, only the initiates that endured the wait patiently were rewarded by receiving the secrets. It was wonderful to see and understand her respect and to proceed from each thing that she would dare hand over as a teaching. To be in her presence with enthusiasm, no drama, with good posture, without complaints, was something that made you feel worthy of you and her. Even if she explained something that you were familiar with, you would show her respect by listening to her once again. She was trying to tell you something.

If you had to leave before completing the activity, you could explain the reasons beforehand, that way she ensured one was focused on her teachings and would then notice you with her eyes on your way out. It would feel like a good-bye that went along with you, and respect back toward her.

In daily life, many of us have the misfortune of seeing the teacher or facilitator waiting for us in the morning when we arrive late. They are the ones that serve coffee, chat and laugh with us. At the end, they would say goodbye and collect the trash that we, the beginners, leave behind.

I like to feel that the Mage was someone special, so humble that she would be the last to arrive; this way the whole group would welcome her. The same thing would happen when she was leaving, everyone would say goodbye. In reality, this whole legacy was fostered by the Mage and was something that made you feel special. Like a Samurai in training within the arts of respect, love and internal strength, without underestimating anything or anyone.

A lot of people approached her after her teachings; in her intolerant tolerance, she would only smile. Some simply wanted her gaze, others her powerful and vast love. Ultimately, this woman was someone so beautiful to witness—and to experience—that no one was capable of summarizing all the reasons for wanting to keep her as close as possible.

I often thought that she didn't exist, as she moved at the speed of light, like an instant ray of love would do.

When someone touches you like this in the mind, you are under a spell that makes you reconsider your own origin.

The waiting continued. I was ready to let time take its course, all the time that was needed for her.

To recall what I had learned thanks to her legacy made me calm down. From time to time, I would say to myself vigorously, "What have you learned and how have you made use of it?"

I had to wait longer even though the night was approaching. The fog began to get more and more dense. In truth, the place was a frightening one. It was almost impossible not to listen to each noise in the not so lonely setting. I felt like everything was amplified in my ears. Raindrops started to fall over the occupied land and I was not familiar with the sensation produced by listening to a heavenly music among the guardian trees. I felt I was in a final judgment.

I didn't know what I had done to deserve this wait—for better or for worse—in that open space. I just knew that I should wait, with courage, for her.

Maga.

Finally, after a long wait, I was distracted and raised my gaze, and saw that she was approaching. Slowly and peacefully she started walking toward me. Her peace enveloped me.

It would be impossible to imagine seeing a ghost and remaining still. I didn't doubt it was she; she would always make me feel that my inner power was possible in her presence. I had to breathe and stay calm; my state of anxiety was evident. The script returned to my memory with purpose:

"Good morning *Maga*, I'm ready to undertake the biggest project that no one has ever propos ..."—Silence—Everything went blank; my words left me. Her being would silence everything that was false. I looked her in the eyes and felt as if my skin had been snatched away. I was mute, and the wind, daring to caress me, made me feel that I was exposed to everything, especially to her.

Slowly, she moved closer. She began to caress the tombstones with her bare long hands in the wet cold. Thanks to the last rays of the sun, the luminous green core of the moss refused to die. I felt the wild animal circle me, stalking me so that I was fearful... I felt under siege, harassed, surrounded. Inviting and seductive words that I could fall into, flat on my face. In this way, with one blow, I would perish in the attack. We were tensed for the duel, paused and observing a great deal. Who would bite first? The beasts could smell themselves, waiting to attack.

This time I was able to anticipate. Very cautiously I began to use her deadly weapon: *silence*. So for some long and endless minutes, we locked gazes, sparring with our eyes. In this spectacle, the surrounding mist played with the dew. The stones, cultured by the silence of wisdom, were determined to give themselves away before the presence of such muteness. In a place where anything could manifest, I could hear a "non-silence" in the absence of the "spell" of spoken words, and I was willing to give up part of what I had learned on my journey so that she would speak to me. I was enveloped in her presence and the dimensions that opened up to me.

When I looked closely at her she seemed like another person, not the same that I expected. Her face pale and cold. Distant, perhaps in another world. I took a breath.

I moved away a few steps; I felt afraid. Nevertheless, I wanted to continue. I began to feel the presence of the elements that surrounded the Mage, her magic was before me.

Small fairies fluttered over her, producing light while she blinked, and she smiled while touching them. The wind was starting to wander around and I could feel it like a waiting companion. The elementals exploited it. The trees that accompanied our steps began to transform into corporeal guardians. Men of astounding spiritual power. The Mage was not alone in the world of silence. I was amazed and undaunted in the face of such a wonder. I felt tremendous gratitude for what I was experiencing ... Sitting and almost delirious with these visions, she came closer to my ear and her voice spoke these pertinent words:

"Today is not the day that I will give you what you most aspire to and want; you will have to wait one year. Then you will live your true initiation if you want to learn from me. Alone and far away from my physical presence, you will obtain that which you don't know about yourself."

She continued muttering as if someone could hear us. Meanwhile, I was paling.

"We'll see each other in Madrid on September 25th, at The Santo Domingo Hotel, close to the Gran Via. There will begin what you and I shall continue from this moment on."

Without further ado, she turned her back to me. The ancient green gravestones at my feet were sending immense waves of dense and freezing cold into my chest. Immediately, something started to stir inside of me. A massive surge made my heart burst from my body. A whole year. A journey, a sequence whose importance only she knew, in order to gain access to the cosmos and the great secrets surrounding her. I followed her at a distance solely with my gaze. I sensed her moving away with firm steps on the ground within the fog, with her black coat and those blessed necklaces that adorned her as if they were the bells of *Creation*.

In her unhurried walk I witnessed how the fairies and the wind were drifting away, levitating her.

"*Maga*. Mystery and enigma of a woman made real that torments me and that I must follow." I told myself.

At the same time, my dreams and expectations of a presumed success had crumbled in a second. I felt a volcano of rage inflaming my veins. I cried, and when I got tired of kicking the emptiness; I sat on a boulder. "Life has to be greater than my rage," I dared to say out loud, as if someone was listening. The stone was cold and slimy; it reminded me of how my heart had been left after this long wait with so many twists and turns.

In my despair I didn't realize that each tombstone, lost in time, had a clear message for me. It was as if the dead were shrieking, a signal that I still didn't want to hear or believe.

For a moment I felt dread. Terrified, I wanted to run from this place, gloomy and dark like my own shadow, when I heard my soul telling me:

"You are stepping on your present time with the past." I held onto one of the generous guardians that quietly allowed me to embrace it.

Time was lost before my presence, silence covered it all. Then I knew that to dream was as real as undertaking a journey.

"*Maga*, are you there?" Silence, darkness and an unknown confidence absent of fear began to emerge.

Everything whispered very clearly, "You know what's coming." The Mage had methods to open portals so that we, the initiated, could enter into them. Activating your wrists, stroking your back with specific and subtle movements. Then she concluded, telling you:

"The locks are open."

She knew and manipulated very precise concepts of sacred trigonometry and its scope. Not to mention what was revealed only to her, which many of us could not dare to imagine.

I began to calm down. Yet I was feeling strange things in my body, as if her mere presence had left the doors ajar to begin walking the unknown. I could see then that which separated me from death: just a few slabs. I was alive. This was something that now I could not, nor should, forget.

This was how this story began. Exactly one year ago and, of course, I have to admit I'm not the same. Now, in silence I understand her ... because I understand myself. I have come to comprehend that I can present myself with more respect; her intention had been to make me understand this. In a few words, I was beginning to have faith.

To be able to decipher her, one has to be a connoisseur—with respect—of life, death and its hidden forces. To be able to describe her—within her world—we must not judge her, since that world is hardly visible.

Much less plausible to us, the obstinate ones, these forces are neglected and weakened, due to our stubbornness and arrogance. I am convinced that this energy is at the level of consciousness that I am at. It is the energy that makes the magic, which you should never question or doubt again.

The Mage now opens portals and at times lets me in, where we can feel that what is yet to be lived is part of a destiny that no one should alter nor influence. These places only give you internal strength to observe, breathe and continue on.

Third path

"The possibility to traverse"

Today was September 25th; at least this is what the calendar marked. I was in Madrid. I set out to our meeting, at the agreed place and the arranged time. I awaited her, this time more calm and centered, for the most part. The hotel where we agreed to meet was very small. Lots of people were walking anxiously about the lobby, paying attention only to their personal affairs. Everything was happening in a tense tranquility. However, I was happy to be there. I trusted and felt worthy of the occasion and my accomplishments. I intended to be very alert upon her arrival, perhaps from the main door, which weighed a ton, being an old building renovated into a hotel. Very attentive, I didn't neglect the elevator exit, in case it brought her from the sky. I had everything covered. Beforehand, I had carefully checked the breakfast area, without any luck. Now, the waiting was more relaxed. I didn't know for sure at what time the Mage might manifest. The chair of the lobby was very comfortable, wide with big cushions of soft silk. I was a bit tired, since the night before I had not slept very well. In the blink of an eye, my eyes closed and I found a place to rest within me. I could feel my saliva dribbling out of my mouth, and perhaps a loud snore woke me up. I was able to smile and continue with my delightful plan to continue resting. I already was in the place on the big day. Everything could be at peace now. A tranquil moment that I enjoyed while waiting.

Agitated, I felt her gaze on my face. I wiped away the drool, and leapt up from my well-deserved break. Her presence was close; I could see her sitting right in front of me. The Mage was there, as she had promised. I restrained myself in order not to run and hug her.

What pleasure and joy I felt in her presence. *Maga*.

For a while, we looked at each other as in a mirror, recognizing us from a place that I have never witnessed. I enjoyed her friendly smile in silence and, in some way, with admiration for being there as agreed. *Maga*.

She was in casual dress. September was a wonderful time to be in Madrid. White shirts and white trousers. Simple and without a lot of noise. She never considered looking different; this was a priority for her. She liked to mingle among people and be nothing. Very sophisticated attire would leave her exposed immediately. When she was working in the initiations, she liked to wear loose and colorful clothing. Each outfit she wore was sacred.

The Mage possessed an eccentric and inevitable look. Whoever recognized her, fell in love. Children identified her immediately, they were more astute and free from judgments and complexes, and so from faraway they noticed her and were drawn to her as if she was a treasure trove or a mountain of toys. Her words were like candies, buoyant like balloons with good intentions.

The elders and wise men recognized her for her wisdom of the soul, and her love reached them from any place she went. While in the lobby, during our acknowledgement, no one could have imagined the reasons behind our exchanging glances.

Her presence was full with an absolute grace for the one who wants to look in a mirror.

The scents and lights that gather around her could take you immediately to your own childhood memories. If she wanted to, she could precipitate any emotion that your heart tried to hide. You might end up crying or in the middle of a senseless laughter. She filled everything: she gifted you with truth, in the mystery of your truth.

The flashy necklaces that she was wearing caught my eye. I couldn't stop looking at them. There was a mix of beautiful blue quartz with pink veins that a shaman, whom she respected and loved very much, had given her. From time to time I had the chance to listen to some stories that the Mage started as tales, full of many fantasies and magical realism.

Whenever she referred to him, I felt love emerging in her voice. From what she told me I got a sense that this travelling companion had decided to return to the sacred mountains to find himself. He was never seen again, this way he ensured that the others could still continue on with learning. Very few dared to enter the mountain. In one of her teachings, the Mage told me that the mountain was our mirror. Few want to know who they are. Snakes were like arrows on the mountain. Anyone who hurt themselves would see snakes along the journey. *Maga.*

She was also wearing a rosewood rosary and a silver chain with a pendant in the shape of a sphere that made sounds when she moved it with the wind of her soul. She would always conceal; it was difficult to see her open up completely. She would leave that task in your hands so that your eyes would hurt from your own light within.

Her blouse, almost a pure white, displayed those "spiritual jewels" as though they were a pretty bow on this gift, which had been introduced into my existence.

After a short time of beholding each other, finally she rushed forward to give me a warm hug. For the first time I felt I was able to receive what the Mage was willing to give me. Now I was worthy of knowing how. With short insightful glances, we prepared to leave the hotel to walk without a destination. I had a profound fear of breaking her silence. The absence of words was like thunderous noise in my soul. She was always and ever that way, tormenting and at times expressing the grandeur of the cosmos.

The Madrid sky obliged the passersby to seek some shade as a protection from its limpid blue, scandalous brilliance. The temperature invited wearing something light. We felt only happiness for our planned reunion. For a long stretch of time we moved around the marvelous Spanish streets. Tourists bustled among the attractions. The gastronomic offerings would attest to their seasoning and the character of the restaurant's premises. We only exchanged glances between shop windows and the commonplace things of life. Mandatory stops would stimulate our appetite between coffees and chocolates. I was experiencing a good time with her. With myself.

Along an endless street, she pointed out the door of the old Carmen Church near the Gran Via. The five o'clock afternoon mass was just starting. We joined in at that precise time, as if God was waiting for her presence to bless her with a ritual, welcoming both of us. I sat next to her. Her connection didn't take long. I was able to observe her closely; I saw how she was moved and shed some very heartfelt tears from the heart. I remembered the meeting at the cemetery and the things that I had witnessed. No doubt a lot was already happening or about to take place.

I wanted only to pay attention and not miss a single moment. Sighing, laughing, desiring, living each outburst as if she maintained a direct communication with something celestial and powerful.

In my desire to witness her being, I could only observe and feel a little of that. Something was telling me that all this transpired time was the best initiation to be able to understand the depth of her absolute magic. The Mage was not a young woman. Nor was she elderly. She was a grown-up girl, however very wise. A sage, as the *Mamos* of the Sierra Nevada of Santa Marta in Colombia would say.

At times, I thought she was a spirit, because I would see her in every corner of my life since I had been exposed to her and her path. She would fill my heart if I thought of her, she caused me to talk with myself and I would argue the matter of wanting to awaken and not knowing how. Her height would stand out from the ordinary. Her skin was fresh, as if of a fallen angel on earth. Her fragile and delicate feet called my attention; it seemed that they had never been set on the ground. At least not these feet that the Mage would show at any instant and in any place, swathed in her beautiful sandals.

Her eyes were brown like the thickest honey, but at the same time they could appear as obscure as a dark night. Looking at them conjured images of the somber color palette that Goya must have used in his black paintings: "Saturn Devouring His Son," "Fight with Cudgels," or maybe "The Fates." Black treasures full of light for the one who dares.

Looking deeper into her eyes, one could observe what it is like to encounter the true windows of the soul; her pupils were that profound and full of feeling.

At the end of the heartfelt ritual, the liturgical service concluded. The event, filled with sacred energy, was ending with a lot of emotion. We were ready to leave the holy place and the Mage allowed me to take her arm. We started walking with a little more confidence, enjoying the company and the feeling of appreciating each other's presence. "It is always good to come to places where people gather in search of miracles and celestial messages," the Mage shared with a clear voice. "Who knows, maybe an angel sees you and gives you a little of his own, simply for being there," she added. I gave her all my attention and I was left feeling only plenitude knowing that, little by little, I was listening to myself.

We agreed that the next stop would be to satisfy our hunger. We ventured out to find the most typical dishes in beautiful Madrid, which still resisted nightfall. The favorite food of the Mage was vegetables, although for obvious reasons she never rejected what was offered. However, I suppose that by being in Madrid she allowed her spirit to be infused with empathy with her surroundings and exclaimed:

"Paella and red wine. Let's enjoy!"

Along the way, the crowd was celebrating the present season of the coming year, benevolent and full of frenzy. A few meters away we found a humble place. With just one look we walked toward it. Cozy tables, a lot of light, and a lot of people that were talking in a deafening manner encompassed the scene. We chose a cozy spot where the noise and the service displayed the energy of that afternoon, filled with the spirit of the "Ole" of Madrid. As we sat down, we were able to breathe and make space for what would be a good and interesting chat between us. Upon ordering, I noticed how the waiter was captivated by the kindness and "grace" of my companion. She was a woman capable of drawing a smile from the most reluctant person.

Frankly, she looked me in the eyes. She asked me again, but this time in a more subtle way:

"What do you want from me?"

I had to regard her with more strength and maturity, without so much fear. I knew what I wanted and now I would go straight to the point.

"You've been with me for a year even though your voice and your presence couldn't reach me. I wonder if you are now able to know what you desire," said the Mage.

My anxiety couldn't be greater. I didn't know how to admire her more than I already did. The conversation was important for me, but I sensed that whatever was about to be discussed, she had already manifested from afar. Still I dared, for this blessed year had given me the best of my life. I felt so much gratitude inside of me. I knew that I couldn't ask for more than what I could see for myself and at times understand.

I looked her in the eyes, breathed in and mumbled some words trying to be as honest as possible with myself:

"*Maga*, this year I have spoken from my heart. This process has been so precious that only now do I see you differently. I now know what I want for myself. I also know what I want from you."

Her face was expressionless. I wasn't expecting anything, since I knew that she understood in some way what I was trying to express. There was silence—she breathed—and I prepared myself for the worst, once again. With her charming joy that filled my life with happiness, she said out loud:

"Do you like rice pudding?"

I burst into laughter and she, grinning, knew it; knew everything. I felt calmed.

I was beginning to understand that it was more than a year ago that I had shared her essence, *"pura vida,"* as they say in beautiful Costa Rica, pure magic. Speechless in that moment, her eyes looked through me and she smiled from her spirit. I was grateful for her kindness, the way it made me feel was worth every second. She listened, attentively and wholeheartedly, to me without saying a word. What an art it is to be able to see from the light within.

With a composed voice and in a plain fashion I began to pose my question:

"I want you to initiate me in your wisdom so that I can capture it in words. I know I can convey your wisdom abroad. The people and the planet should know about you. As you say, learning should go faster in less time, and at the least cost.

So ... a book, *Maga*, let me write one about you. I know you take from the cosmos, you talk to something superior and, even then, you remain ordinary and simple, your echoes end up being rations of consciousness. I love you and want you in writing," I declared.

The silence supported everything that was unfolding. She stared at me somewhat strangely. I held my breath. Her gaze was insisting. What do you want from me? I started giving a thousand answers, distressing myself and thought:

—Whatever it is, she is all of it.

She interrupted my thoughts at the precise moment that I found the necessary space for gratitude that she was there.

She took my hands and held them for a long time. I felt so loved and acknowledged, inevitable tears fell over the furrows of my life.

"Beloved woman, I'm not a writer. I only know that the words that are close to Him are the ones we should understand. You do your work and I do mine. This way we are both with Him." There was a pause and we had time to savor all that was said.

After a few minutes, our palates were presented with the celebration of the day, the rice pudding of Madrid. Upon seeing it, she exclaimed, "This is life, the rest can wait!" Then, in a calm voice, she added, "Life is something tragic or sweet, it all depends on what one wants to eat."

At that point, I tried to present a business opportunity between us, a partnership. I think I had started to lose another battle. Perhaps my proposal was too mundane for the Mage. She knew the beginning and the end as a totality, of the alliances, of the methods, rituals, paths and legends. Between spoonfuls, she told me with a taste of sweetened milk:

"You must be alive to write. I do not have anything to say, you can only live it to write it."

Then I understood the challenge facing a person that doesn't stockpile past or future, because their seeds are everywhere. What was important was to just be bones.

She looked into the distance and paused for a while. It seemed that she was searching for information and it was taking longer to reach her. I observed her only with respect, awaiting whatever it might be. I knew what respect meant.

Out of nowhere she looked at me and said, without pausing and with a lot of enthusiasm:

"Tomorrow I'll wait for you at Barajas airport. We'll leave at 10 in the morning via Zurich. Find a ticket. You're coming with me. We're going to live while you write ..."

I couldn't speak. A turmoil of sobbing, emotion and fear came up in procession. Her face showed pleasure at seeing me in temporary madness at what she had given me.

She was enjoying her magic and the results. Now that it was a reality, she added, "What are you going to do?" She was laughing hard, very hard, with a hysterical laughter. *Maga.*

With no budget or pretension, I was brimming with adventure and initiation. My trip was just beginning. I would be accompanied by my smile that was beginning to bear life.

She said nothing else. She slipped away, looking full of enthusiasm, alive and ecstatic about administering journeys. For a moment I sat there without moving. The waiter barged in on the event of my soul and said:

"The bill."

In my wallet full of mysteries, I looked for the coins that would assure me the path toward the Mage. The best coins are those that have two sides, hence the wealth of the soul. Now all of them were important.

Even though I was walking through a river of people, it was as though I was alone. No one could understand what I felt at this moment: fortunate, doubtful, fearful, joyful. All this I felt with a previously unknown intensity, because I was living them for the first time at a different level.

I was overwrought by my thoughts again, like a bomb ready to detonate.

Pack, call home and let them know that you will leave the following day, but ... When would I return? Projects, plans that add up to a one-way ticket and the courage to return. I'm leaving with the Mage and her wishes became indications. *Maga.*

My heart knew for a year its dream, its course. Now it was a reality, there was no time to lose. Here I would go—from cemeteries toward life and the return.

Suddenly I saw myself alone, without knowing what airlines or flight I should take. My heart was saying, "Cheer up, it's only the greatest dream you have ever achieved."

Here we go again. Now I believed in that round-trip ticket. It was the journey toward *La Maga* ...

Fourth Path

"Arriving"

My heart arose shaken today. I had a premonition. I still did not understand what it was, but I was certain that more changes were coming, since I went from tears to a strange happiness and went on not knowing why. Before I was feeling what I felt now, no person or situation would generate this fearful and divine pleasure in me.

I felt that my love came from a place that I didn't dare to say that I knew. She, the Mage, always talked about the "teacher": the heart, and this was the only thing that made sense to me in these circumstances in which all of this was unfolding.

The doors that my "teacher" had opened were starting to be celestial gates on earth. Everything else could wait while I enjoyed the wonder of not bypassing my feelings. Without delusions. What I had been responsible for concluding all these years, was starting to take place.

I was falling in love with me. It was undeniable. I maintained a feeling of joy deep inside, in that constant pulse of living one second at a time. I didn't have dreams or expectations. The best was already happening to me. I started savoring the phrase. One day at a time. I finished packing and left early for the airport into the most delicious madness I was about to undertake.

I got carried away and, as if under a spell, I obtained everything (or what was necessary) to accompany her and her journey. She would leave everything to the greater tests. That which was for you, was for you. Destiny did not recognize time. Most of the time we were in silence.

The waiting area was somewhat empty for a flight that was full of passengers. I walked restlessly back and forth, while she enjoyed her own company, sitting on her chair. They gave the boarding call. Once we were in our own seats, it took little time before the Mage fell into a deep sleep. In this way I was able to recount my life events and what I had dared to do.

I could see her; I was with the Mage on a plane. Was this a dream? At this time I said to myself, "One day I will write about this experience."

The flight was quiet and peaceful. Sitting near the window I could see beautiful mountains and snowy peaks to the right of the plane. Something made me feel special and I couldn't describe what I was experiencing. I was feeling the movement of life next to me. We arrived in Zurich at the scheduled time, and claimed our luggage without any inconvenience. The Mage travelled light.

Up to this point I had let myself be completely carried away by the Mage. We walked out the door that would lead us to the train station. Along the way a handsome man joined us, over 50 years of age, which he carried graciously. He was another of her initiates, who came to welcome the Mage. She noticed my look of interest. She looked at me and remarked in a humorous way, "Don't be so surprised, all the disciples are the same."

I looked at her, puzzled, not understanding her comment, or perhaps playing dumb after being exposed.

When she saw my reaction, she said: "If you truly aspire to be a teacher, you should remember one of the core ideas: never lose the sense of humor."

She was witty and whimsical. You never knew if she was talking seriously. You had to be alert. Everything was serious with her.

"He," she said pointing at him, "is a little further ahead of you, but not by much." She said this while letting out an ironic laughter. Inevitably, we started to laugh uncontrollably. This was how I met the Mage's initiate. A special being.

Upon our arrival I was moved to see that the initiate had many offerings for the Mage. To my surprise she received with joy all that he offered. It was obvious he felt gratitude for what the Mage had given him by exchange of knowledge. Among magicians and apprentices there were many codes to follow, debt should never accumulate. Owing amongst them was risky, it weakened the magic. "To owe a magician weakens your enchantment," I heard her say many times. It was what happened when one did not understand the magic of love and respect.

"There is nothing like acknowledging the other," the Mage always said. "It is the only way that they grant you tools for your own protection."

I imagined that it meant something about the respect we must feel for the destiny of anyone who enters our lives.

We were all perfect in essence; the hardest thing was to claim the essence.

Her initiate-companion escorted us to the place where another woman was waiting to greet the Mage in another designated location. I must confess that I was glad for the presence of our guide, because the Mage was fully enjoying her trip and trusting the sun that was shining on her.

While the initiate was buying the tickets for our trip, we waited together in silence. However, from a distance I noticed how the initiate observed the Mage with eyes full of light and great pride, in a kind and respectful way. I liked how he looked at her. We both felt as if the Mage was full with seeds and our task was to take care of and plant them very soon.

They had known each other for a while now. The Mage had split his soul in two to let in the light of life. Now he was one of those that wanted her experience, legacy and, at times, her power. The Mage was very reserved and careful in her demeanor.

Her greatest talent was to know beforehand, to anticipate: how, where, when, what or with whom. She could get very close and know your shortcomings and voids, yet the best thing was that she knew the intentions of people before they were able to notice. What she most rejected was the selfish type of person, not valuing respect, and the renowned seducers trying to divert her from her path. She avoided the ones that boasted about knowledge, with diminutive heart. She did not tolerate cunning people that were incapable of cooperating to allow her to pass or to remain next to them. She would surrender in the presence of honesty, it aroused her true fascination.

If someone expressed their truth to her, she would remain attentive, breathe and then would fly away. She loved the simplicity of the just, no matter how cruel. Liberation without blame. The freedom of the hidden truth within, obscured by one's own delusions.

I remember one day in an activity with the initiated. She brought a plate of provisions and offerings to Mother Earth, and placed it in a visible place for everyone. One of the participants walked by and took a good chunk of chocolate from the tray. As the ceremony began and she listened to the first words of the Mage, the girl with the audacity realized the significance of that ritual. She felt very ashamed for ignoring that the offering that she had taken belonged to a sacred act. She then looked at the Mage with the courage to accept her infraction with responsibility, but she only observed her back with a look of love and understanding. So much so that she felt forgiven for what had happened. Both ended up laughing for that mischief as if they were two child accomplices, witnesses to something marvelous. If only we could be kids and just smile before so much pretense accumulated inside of us.

Nevertheless, one day the Mage told me, "The truth sets you free and is also dangerous. Too much light is not advisable for anyone." Until this day, this still resonates with me and antagonizes me. Something so deep and complex, you can only live it to grasp it. In this way she initiates you and will leave you under the spell of your own life. That is her, truly transparent. Being in her presence makes you explore yourself and be shaken, until you finally are able to know yourself in front of that mirror of a thousand pieces, scattered in your own presence.

We managed to get on board pretty quickly at the central station, and then proceeded toward the small village of Lützelflüh. I observed how the Mage and her initiate, who had kindly helped lead her to the final destination, related in encoded words. Knowledge, experiences, questions and answers filled the coach, pointing toward the light. At times she was silent, though the conversation was still taking place, in another plane. He opened the pockets of his soul and was taking in the flow of what she was exchanging with wisdom.

The exchange was of semblances, of life and words. One could only observe in silence. Nothing else to do. Everything was done.

Faraway we could see a small town welcoming us with its greenery and marvelous architecture. Our final destination was close and, little by little, I was feeling the exhaustion of the long day. Finally the train arrived at the tiny station.

We took our luggage. When we opened the doors we celebrated the pure air of the mountain. We started to walk among a crowd that was just returning from their workday in the larger cities. Gradually the station was left deserted. We noticed that an elderly and wise woman was trying to catch up with us. The Mage was very happy to see her. Both maintained a long embrace as only two enlightened women could do. The silence of that hug indicated the respect they had for each other. The initiate companion was delighted to see these two powerful beings. He exalted in his supportive role, tasked with safely taking the Mage to the place where she would do her work in the coming weeks.

The time came to say goodbye. The Mage looked at her initiate with strength. He could not contain himself and embraced her with such gratitude that my heart felt as if it would explode with emotion. In that moment I thought that, sooner or later, I would confront the same thing that I was witnessing tearfully. I had to find inner strength. Separate from her? I did not want to think about it for now.

She looked at him. I heard when she said, pointing at his chest:

"Take care of my heart. I am taking care of yours."

That was a deep yet simple code that revealed sparks of the initiation.

We said goodbye, recognizing each other in our specific roles, so that the Mage would be able to fulfill her mission in each leg of the journey. I can't deny that after saying goodbye to him in the station, I was left with a feeling that we would see each other many times in a not so distant future. It was ok to say goodbye.

Setting out in an old and dirty car, a man was at the wheel and drove it like a sports car on the racetrack. The Mage was chatting with the wise woman and the car was going up and down without much caution. The initiate-guide made the return trip to Zurich's airport where he would be reunited with his family for a long trip to Cape Verde. It seemed then that everyone was in their place, except my stomach, which wanted to purge its contents thanks to the driver and the curves. *Maga* ...

The Mage ignored me and most of the time did not introduce me as her traveling companion. At times I felt that this woman would scarcely show herself, and now my being, in her dimension, inhabited the same space. It was fine this way, little by little I was understanding why she allowed herself to be seen and what her purpose was.

Her walk was keen and discreet. I knew that she had the capacity to transform into a powerful wild animal and would, simply, wait until the prey was closest to annihilate it. My fears were letting me see such realistic images in her presence, that I was moved by their effect.

My task was to follow her and write about her, that's the reason I was with her. We were about to create something. Next to her, I let myself be carried away through a dark street filled with rusty doors ready to be opened.

There was a great silence along the way, despite the loud engine noise. Nevertheless, there was peace. It was something magical. The mountains embedded into the landscape were showcased among the flowers and the beauty of the place.

In the distance, the ringing bells of a small church were announcing that the cosmos knew of the arrival of the Mage. Everything was in order for Mother Earth, for her, and now for me.

A few miles away you could see the place that would welcome the Mage and her presence. She had already been in these lands in previous years, teaching strength and knowledge. Everyone was waiting for her in the prepared space, where she would lay her dreams each night and would allow the essence of her cosmic presence to be revealed.

A small road, embedded among the colors and aromas, displayed cobwebs like rainbows. The snow at the top of each majestic mountain would invoke calm in anyone. My eyes presented me with a landscape that moved me and I felt so exhilarated; perhaps this was the way the Mage experienced her inner world. The external world that was bestowed by being connected with the wonder of that which is internal: the roots, the mountains, life ... Maybe God.

She had the knowledge. I was aware of that. I could only observe and wait patiently, never an art for me. What essentially united me with this woman was soon to be discovered. What I was living was the book that I had to deliver.

At the bottom of the hill, after many curves in the long journey from the train station, I saw the magical place that was welcoming the Mage to do her work. At the end of a pathway, was a beautiful home, perhaps 100 years old; the beginning of another path. Gardens filled with multicolored flowers on display, nurseries housing plants, and a small establishment where we could get fruit jams and a variety of small leaves turned into beverages. The foliage that was covering the beautiful place was displaying less vibrant shades, since fall was giving way to the coming winter. Oranges, violets and yellows, all together, were dressing up the high walls of the house. The tree knew of the seasons and its will would soon give way to the new one. Life regenerates; the seasons give us clues to the inner processes. In her teachings, the Mage would make you feel vital and constant. Something similar to the inner world is found in images of nature. Mother Earth invented the four seasons so that things did not happen all at once. Thereby she would teach us with the most everyday and ordinary things. I was left mesmerized and wondered if I was in spring, where everything was reborn. Perhaps winter, where restlessness was reflected in my short patience to wait out the thaw.

"You have to be a seed, wait in the darkness and soon you will become fruit." How could one not understand this phrase so deep and true?

La Maga. How could one not feel her now, when she was right before your eyes?

At every opportunity, I tried to capture her dimensions in my notes. Until, little by little, I became aware that, more than understanding them, I had been living them for some time.

She opened the door and walked toward the assigned place for her to rest. I dared to follow her and knew that she could feel my presence. I knew now that this was okay.

A narrow hallway with a staircase took us to the room of the Mage. We climbed the stairs with some difficulty, trying not to trip over our luggage.

Upon entering her room, she immediately walked to the terrace that presented the afternoon blush, fading with a gentle rosy breeze. Dusk was settling and transforming into thousands of colors fused with the landscape of the mountain. Life was about to enter stillness. With nightfall everything was in balance. I couldn't contain my amazement when I saw that her bed was positioned below the space in the ceiling that had only transparent glass. Exactly under the sky.

Even the ceiling revealed her presence. I could imagine her sleeping and waking up with the stars and the dawn fully above her.

The double bed was tucked in with a down duvet that invited you to jump on it. Large pillows and cushions with blankets of bright and vivid colors made this place the perfect accommodation.

On the right side of the room there was a small table that had been adorned with flowers and peculiar fruits to make the Mage feel welcome.

Everything was unique. The place where the Mage would sleep, her dreams and her realities had been witnessed by me.

Once more impressed, I left in silence, leaving her alone where she was available for everyone. I liked that idea that she was treated in this way: simply, but always with the best and most magical.

Living in such simplicity, this place would make any human being wish for the stars that would be part of their journey in the coming nights.

My room was two levels below hers. There was enough distance to realize that she was the one closest to the source of *God*.

My place was austere, as was everything I had to learn with the Mage. A small bed very well-dressed and simple. The bedside table with a lamp that would allow me to read. Just enough space to place my luggage. At that moment, with a roof and a bed, everything was known and must be revealed. I felt complete and full of gratitude. I had the essentials and I liked the modesty of the place.

I was tired. I organized my things and embarked on the path toward my dreams, those that allowed me to carry on when I was awake.

Before going to sleep that night, I thought about each thing that I had experienced. I started to imagine the Mage under the stars. In prayer, perhaps. Her life filled with spiritual tools, her capacity to bring the teachings to places and people that would become apprentices in the face of her wise and loving power.

Fifth Path

"Cable to earth"

I opened my eyes; I noticed the light coming through the window and into the terrace of my room. I assumed it was the sunrise by the quality of the light. I got up somewhat confused, for a moment I did not know where I was. It took me some time to recall that I was in this old house, in this beautiful place and that the Mage was sleeping near me.

The evening had done me a courtesy by means of the silence and the freshness of the morning. I had the feeling of a solitary and peaceful time approaching.

The cold air of the mountain entered through every corner. It was more agreeable to open the doors of the small terrace and breathe. For a moment I stared blankly, just feeling and perceiving the place that was changing with the morning light. Suddenly I had the need to investigate this place. I reviewed my notes, that until this moment I had not organized. I still had not written about the experience with the initiate and our trip on the train.

I waited for a prudent hour when I might hear the sounds coming from the main dining room of the house where we were staying. The only thing that I wanted was coffee, sacred medicine. My everyday relationship with this magic potion is something that I should consider soon. I ought to write a book titled *Death by coffee*. Its aroma, composition, so full with stimulants, was the best thing to wake up to, besides life.

I have bought it in the places that I have visited. I liked coming back home and having coffee from the special place where it was cultivated. I was an expert in recognizing a good coffee. It opened me up to the land and its origins, that primitive Africa. The warriors of that continent were treated as such by benefiting from daily doses to maintain strength and stamina. Pope Clement VIII himself resolved to try coffee. While savoring it, he said, "This Satan's drink is so delicious, it would be a pity to let the infidels have exclusive use of it. We shall fool Satan by baptizing it and this way we'll make it a truly Christian beverage."

Its fragrance beckoned me to the daily pleasure of life. Coffee— full of shadows and sins till its end—It was almost a messenger.

While I was finding my way toward this *pleasure*, I stumbled into a man who showed me the route to the treasure I sought. There, in that unexpected impact, we collided with each other and with the *Beloved*, God itself …

It was *undeniable* that this man that enlivened me, together with the coffee, performed some activity within the place. What distinguished him was a white apron he wore with a lilac flower pattern in the center, which disclosed the name of the small place prepared for breakfast.

His hair, wavy, long and black, captivated me more than any other thing in the place. His eyes were penetrating and invited me to conquer life itself. He was handsome, with tanned skin. Of fine bearing. The confidence with which he moved and what he radiated left me totally enchanted. An enigma calling me.

Immediately we both intuited a dance that we began to recognize. I didn't want our connection to be so evident, but there was no time to lose in denying it.

I was paralyzed by what I felt in the presence of that man.

I managed to make it to a corner sofa, the principle feature of the dining room. An antique that honored the years of the house in a magnificent and classic way.

My tongue was melting on the rim of the cup. Between the coffee and desire, I got carried away. I could only swallow sip by sip without thinking anything else.

I was still wearing my pajamas. Something very simple made of cotton and purple in color. I felt comfortable in the house, and most of the guests were seen in comfortable clothes for the activities offered in the house. Once I was cozy on the couch, I started to look at the man that had stunned me without warning.

It seemed we both were engaged in a ballet of glances. The images in my head played out with no limits; the female, who resisted the male before taking her and, even in physical pain, experienced the pleasure of something so basic and primal. She allowed the brute force to create life without much questioning.

Each of my pores started to feel thirsty. My nipples were upright, beyond any control. My heart was pounding and there, between my legs, I could feel the reason for existence without question or pretention. I was licking the cup and it was caressing me back. Coffee made me like a warrior and stimulated the desire to give myself to the brute force of the stranger.

He turned his body toward me. Smiling, he held his breath and asked me the last thing I wanted to think about:

"Are you with *La Maga?*"

I had to take a stride away from the man with a start that revealed my surprise at the question that nearly took my breath away. For a moment I didn't want to know anything about her or have anything to do with her; I longed to be free in body and soul. Now I was feeling trapped, torn in two directions. My dreams, cut short by desire, were starting to conflict before me.

My name, origin, or anything that had to do with me was diminished before the absolute and important presence of the Mage. I felt like a substitute, an imposter, and absurd. I was only accompanying the most fascinating woman and absolute master of the place. I still had not lived and learned enough to know why this beast would devour me with his eyes.

Up to this point, everything I had programmed myself with had to do with the Mage, always the Mage. I held back the usual rage.

Stunned by that question, now I was disoriented in the face of a possible rival.

I wanted to crawl out of my skin, to understand life and be free from the Mage. I was very afraid of the realm that I was entering.

Was this part of her so called initiation? The onset of the questions began nonstop.

Would this man be in the exclusive service of the Mage? I wanted to know every detail, every move. I was in danger of entering a "risk" zone. Now audacity had entered my soul and I could sense it. A risk that I should take as the mature woman that I supposedly was. Immediately, I went back to my own story: a marriage or relationship that I lost due to my poor disposition. The spectrum of wounds that showed up in a heartbeat, from the past to the present, was an affirmation of the terrain that I was trying to conquer.

During all these years, the most difficult ones to bear the responsibility of had been *betrayal* and *infidelity*. Who was I in this moment to talk or preach of what made me a *sinner*?

As an empty woman knowing very little of her internal strength, I attempted to betray myself, together with some strokes of infidelity. At times I felt victorious and proud. At other times, dirty and unsatisfied. With time I was able to understand; "When I betrayed myself, everyone betrayed me."

In seconds, all of this spilled over my life and my past, but most of all over my present, which insisted on healing by filling me with ambition.

My children were brought into the flow of life. Two beautiful kids. Legacies that life had placed like an order in a department store. It seemed as though life and my inexperience played out despite not being fully present. Even so, I raised them, and the key to everything was to love and respect their father.

In this way, I avoided the disgrace of wasting their time, of having to come to the aid of one of us. At least I was able to do something; I knew for a long time that blame didn't bring solutions. Talking to my offspring about the magical moment when I met their dad was the best thing I ever did. Today I'm certain that he loved me as much as I was not able to love myself. I was looking after other things that had to be taken care of by a woman, in order to awaken and to understand what love is.

Make sure you love the ones who love themselves, was one of the grand truths that I learned from the Mage. I felt fortunate. My heart would fill with gratitude when I thought of their father; I was very fond of that love. I honored it because I understood that our children were the fruit of both of us. Understanding that no separation was possible for us in this life by their mere existence, had made me a kind and harmonious being. However, this relationship with the father of my kids was always lacking something. When you run out of resources, you ask to be relocated. "What is consumed is what can be changed," the Mage would say.

Waiting for a whole year to travel with the Mage, there were nuances of the things that had always happened to me, to the extent that I ended up in the same situations. I was aware that they repeated over and over because I never confronted the things. I always wanted more, just a little more from people whom I demanded to fill up each of my empty spaces, which were the result of believing I could "not" take care of myself.

In the state I was in, I began to question myself if, once more, I wanted to snatch from her the same thing that I had managed to take from other people.

Back in the present and snapping out of the thoughts that continued torturing me, I returned to my coffee and to this sexual beast in front of my sexuality, pulsing like a drum. It was moving, looking at me and I couldn't define it. I knew and sensed that it was sacred to the Mage. The intuition of a woman was something to be wary of, especially if two women were looking for the same thing in a man.

To us females, we are not concerned with a man as such. When another woman comes into play, we only covet the power that accompanies this adversary. We prefer the option of external fighting and avoid at all costs the internal one. Therefore, the best thing is to crush her so that she cannot harm us in the future. Taking her out of the game transforms into pleasure that makes us forget what, in reality, we actually want. Everything with the Mage was about respect. As a consequence, neither of us could take a position at this moment.

Then, who was who in relation to the Mage? What was waiting for me, along this path with its shadows, to begin reconsidering about my assignment?

The coffee won the race to my darkness. I needed to hold onto something until I could reveal what was fueling this path.

Deep down, what gave life to this *delicious specimen* and his female full of desire, was knowing that I was his bounty, loving his lure that was already ensnaring me in pleasure.

Sixth Path

"In the pathway of the skin"

After the encounter, and still stunned by the shimmer in my eyes, I went up to my room for a moment to refresh my soul, to soften it with time. I was happy and excited by my blunder. I decided to change out of my pajamas and put on a pair of jeans and a floral print shirt. Once I tidied myself and felt more calmed, I went down slowly to the breakfast area, knowing that each step I descended was a step toward heaven. I took the door leading between the rooms and the restaurant area, where I continued searching for an outcome to this experience.

Surprise, awe and bewilderment. Someone get me out of here. As I reached the breakfast area there, near the sofa, the coffee and the source of my palpitations, the Mage was sitting in front of what I had declared my territory.

The connection between them immediately moved me, stirring up old internal struggles and debris that still existed somewhere inside, and surely, needed cleansing. They saw me and smiled between them. I had the feeling of knowing they were observing me from a distance, certain that I was not a safe port.

I tried to disguise myself with my best posture and an attitude of "there's nothing going on here; I also don't care, since I don't accept responsibility for anything."

I wanted to camouflage myself with the table. The delicacies on display were a beautiful torment. I would have preferred not to be seen, to be a Kafkaesque insect on top of the bread rolls. None of what was happening should have occurred; my intention of not being seen exposed me from any hiding place. I tried to focus on the feast laid out for the delicious breakfast where I could fill up my hands and my tongue with what I wanted: seasonal fruits, jams, rolls, oatmeal, exotic seeds … aromas and delicacies that delighted my eyes with the promise of their exquisite flavor. I didn't want anything else in this moment but to taste the sweet and sharp desires of that man that was now looking to the Mage's eyes. Little by little I was able to focus on my plate, full of colors. Seeking calm, I started to process and be coherent of the situation that I was living. Minutes passed, and they were lost in that space that one cannot comprehend from the outside. They were cherishing stories and anecdotes that I couldn't begin to suspect. At times I felt ignored, abandoned, expelled from paradise. However, to now abandon every possibility before such a delicious feast was something that I had to refuse.

I could only hold my cup and my gaze. For a long time, I let myself be carried away by a fit of rage for knowing myself a loser. Nonetheless, confronting this situation made me reflect on it more and more. I wanted to stop being compulsive and tediously hurt.

I held my breath. I was letting it all find a space within me. Gradually I was grateful to leave the situation behind and not have to deal with any casualties in this matter. The man was with the Mage and I had to respect that space. For the first time since our encounter with the coffee, I felt like laughing. Sin.

Sinner. I started to laugh and recall the stories of coffee amidst war and pleasure.

This was the only way to weave together the steps within the soul.

The Mage noticed everything that was happening. Who could provoke the wisdom of this woman? How to deceive her? I was starting to feel that I shouldn't deceive myself anymore. I raised my gaze and, when I came across her eyes at length, we looked at each other with tenderness and intensity. There was no need to talk. Everything was intertwined between us. It was possible to converse in silence.

When I thought that I was safe and returned to my old sofa, determined to carry on, I noticed that the walking wonder was approaching me. He came closer and asked me for space to sit next to me.

Some of his co-workers were taking a break from their duties. In an instant, we were all together sharing individual stories and anecdotes. His legs were brushing against mine and it was impossible not to feel his presence. The Mage had flown without me even noticing, in a flash she was gone from the table where she had taken breakfast. I recalled her allied smile and it soothed me. The ultimate rule: keep a sense of humor in the face of any emergency.

Between laughter, coffee and cheer, the man whom a few seconds before I had given up on, was assaulting my senses with his sandalwood and myrrh aroma. His voice stuck to my skin like honey. Long abandoned drums were rumbling once again.

He put his arm over my shoulder and I heard him say to me, through my heightened senses, "At six thirty this afternoon, I will pick you up so you can see the temple where my house is."

I turned my head. Smiling in his eyes and, after a long pause, I said, *"I will be ready, waiting for you."*

The conflict of my weapons and shields was beginning to belong to me. The initiation had started with a major storm: *La Maga*, the setting and the mane of life, set out sturdy nets to catch my impulses of appetite and passion.

After breakfast, everyone set out to their tasks of the day. The hours passed by within me through the old hourglass, this time made of stone.

I was aware of each passing second; the hand of the clock in the main room wrought my soul. Throughout the whole day, I tried to establish some clue or idea to the origin of the one with the divine eyes.

I wanted to speak with the Mage, but my stories of "betrayal" and "fear" were showing themselves once more. Maybe I was scared, now more than ever, of violating something greater; the conviction of knowing that I was pursuing something that might not belong to me.

I was a broken mast on a sailboat that would soon approach a storm called *life*.

The Mage commenced her activities with the newly initiated. She would create rituals, sing and rattle her rain stick. Listening to her was to be near the joyful sound that seeds make when they reach fertile soil. For my part, I was now a sound and, simultaneously, the most fertile soil that I could ever be.

At times you could also see her with a pipe, a treasure given to her by her friends from faraway lands. This wonderful gift would assemble in two parts (feminine and masculine). The female part was a piece of aquamarine granite, very heavy, with embedded moons and stars of bright white to make it more beautiful. A hole represented the darkness, profound and enigmatic, of the female element. In this part, you could place the zest of the tobacco leaf to make smoke that connected with the cosmos. From the hole in the female part a space opened up to assemble with the masculine. The external, the phallus, the weapon, war, what is erect. A long piece of resistant and very hard wood. By the time the Mage assembled this representation of the universe, you could feel the energy that made this pipe sacred. Its cover was made of fabrics with symbols. Fish and one white female bear swaddled it like a coat when it was not being used. It had her name, engraved by her friends. The Mage looked after her tools, especially those considered ancestral. The pipe had been the gift of an aboriginal wise woman, from the area of Ottawa in Canada. It had been made just for her by the community artisans.

The music, dance and the initiate states of everything around us, gave us no time to think or question anything or anyone. From my beginnings on those paths, my life was never again the same. Now I could observe how, doing what was appropriate with the new arrivals, their lives were transforming into magical awareness.

The Mage continued opening portals on her journey. In these you would be immersed despite your stubbornness or struggle. I am talking about a life that, in essence, should never again be dormant nor separate. The Mage had the ability to awaken in you everything you had not learned, until it was transformed into new seeds for sowing.

One had to be able to absorb a lot and then later discard without compassion. I was trying to find a moment alone with her, where I could ask her about this subject of "man." Perhaps this time it would be an ordinary matter. An issue to be addressed between us.

I imagined myself in a storm with him, after losing myself in the presence of the Mage by claiming to take what belonged to someone else. The hours passed, drop by drop of destiny. Doubts assaulted me; the hell of uncertainty was leading me toward the flame of the delicious sensation of victory, pleasure and seduction. This assured me of the change in the path that would transpire.

The power of those eyes captured in the window of my heart made me seek the sun with desperation. Romantic thoughts went back and forth at every moment.

I made the decision to quiet my soul before the Mage. This renewed woman, apparently committed, who also wanted to live part of her destiny with responsibility.

Now I was assuming beforehand the possible consequences of my acts, since I wanted to live the chaos that I had never allowed myself.

At home I was always the complacent girl, to obtain the love that I could not get any other way. I wasn't stupid; I knew that what I was getting into was part of what I was wagering in order to grow. To feel some chaos would help me a lot in what I was plotting, to know myself free in the decisions I would take. Good or bad, they were mine and only mine.

I had a premonition: I would make the Mage understand that I had found an independence and happiness outside of her, far from her world. Despite this, I felt that every step I was starting to take was coming from an unknown place. *Being responsible for my life was a serious and urgent matter.*

As for my assigned task up to that point, it was clear that I should transcribe all the work done by the Mage. In this way I would accomplish a feeling of fulfillment.

I thought I was deceiving myself. The truth of hiding was devouring me inside. Guilt was mocking me and my thoughts were not compassionate, in agony of knowing that I was once again the villain of the story.

How could I look her into her eyes and tell her that in a few hours I would be with her ocean, her sky or her earth? Doubtless, I didn't know what this man represented in the life of the Mage. I could have been honest and asked, but I was afraid of not tasting the forbidden, with the certainty that it was possible to lose it all with my eyes open this time. I liked the idea and it excited me.

Again, filled with courage to force myself to be responsible, sensing the seduction of the first mortal step in the face of the ability to change and be different, confused and ready to go through whatever it was, I climbed the stairs of the old house.

I noticed the brightness of the hallway lights intensifying with every step I would take. The idea of seeing myself illuminated more each time made me feel that the signals were on my side. Walk and keep walking to learn. This filled up the sacred vessel, my body, more than my desire to pursue the Mage or to ever transcribe her.

Time was getting closer; the minute hands had been allies and kind with the time and my emotions. Once in the shower, I was able to feel the agitation, the exaltation for that man that already was a proposition of skin. Enticed under the warm water, I scanned my body with my hands that knew by heart the road to reach solitary pleasure.

I examined my body and the sacred routes. I had to know at this moment that the outcome of the night would be to make a decision about the path of fear. A former comrade of many. Fear. Shadow that makes any form of love recoil. Crippler of stories and tales. Snake that goes weaving a path that we start to transit by memory to ensure the preservation of life. Detestable fear, you had made me love you despite so many things. Today I had the desire to overcome my former companion; today was about decision and courage.

Today was today.

An empty life, full with dissatisfactions, resulted in poor knowledge of the vessel that contained this woman loaded with complexes and frustrations that I was.

I always wanted to know more about love, to discover the magic of the unseen, about sex as integral to a connection to the higher plane and as a door to heaven. I had spent more time making men believe that my squeals during the carnal act and different forms of pleasure, worked swiftly so that they summarized the sexual act to its most expeditious, and this way I could flee from my desires.

In a nutshell, the faster a man would finish, the less pleasure I would experience.

I remained inside my fantasies that concealed the intimate secrets of being me. I could not trust anyone with my secret pleasures, when the reputation of the good and decent woman was at stake. The complacency reenacted a story; to discover myself was urgent. I knew that, in time, I would find a man that would uncover me playing inside erotic labyrinths where I was sheltering my loyal, unshakeable and hidden self. Once again, tortured by desire, I knew that this night would answer all of my questions because it was what I desired.

At times I thought of the Mage, on her path and what she was doing in this moment. I came back to myself; I wanted to change the way I looked, but couldn't define the type of date. Casual? Open? Selfless? Seductive? Perhaps this was an event that knew no attire.

The Mage assailed me without notice, with thoughts and doubts. A thousand times I repeated to myself: "She already knows of this encounter." Between the sky and the earth there are no secrets. We are all connected somehow. We are here to push or be pushed; how to deny what had been learned and act like a dumb and innocent girl again.

The soul knew, it did not allow itself to be deceived. If it happens in one place, certainly it must be happening in another. I knew this by heart. We are all one. We think we can outwit the other. In fact we deceive ourselves each time we do.

As I mentioned before, I was a devotee of the arts that helped you open the heart, at any cost. It wasn't in vain, all that I had done with myself to be a better person. Each morning, I contemplated how to get out of the trap that I had built, from fearing to live responsibly for what I wanted and what made me happy. As a daily practice, every minute I asked myself: "What makes me happy? Does this make me happy? Does that make me happy?" And this way, little by little, one day I started to say to myself: "I believe so."

I'm certain it did. Slowly I started to feel and to live that which I wanted to learn.

I had been exposed over many years to all kinds of formulas that could shed light to heal my wounds, those that prevented me from enjoying the life outside the prison that we learn to be fearful of.

Each time that it occurred to me to make a mental review of the entire journey, I had a hearty laugh at myself.

Ultimately, we are in these planes to learn. Almost always we choose the most painful one, this way we can be certain that we took the best of the paths. I had the courage to initiate myself in many paths. When none were enough, I thought the next might be better. Over the years, I realized that they were condemned to failure if I didn't act upon what was learned along the way.

For a long time, I thought that others were responsible for my misfortune. For years, I waited for them to change.

Fortunately, I realized that it was no accident that, by lingering in my emptiness, I could only ever attract the same thing. I would end up filling the void from the outside, never from within.

Nevertheless, it had been worth every second. Though it had been tough, now that things passed and made me grow, it had begun to be fun. At times I tell myself that I like to find the difficult route, that I like to grow. I discovered that the hard thing is to live and the most comfortable thing is to quit. No one suspects that, when we are about to quit, we are but one small step from *God*.

The forces of life are almost indecipherable. *This thing of being alive is a serious matter!*

At first the processes started by the external: the body, the appearance, the sacred vessel, the temple, what the majority sees from the outside. The boundary between what separates light from darkness, the skin and the spirit, we could say.

I never felt attractive. I was never satisfied with myself. At the beginning there were diets, reducing massages, minor surgeries, a lot of sun to achieve tanned and tempting skin and a lot of exercise— the one activity that took much of my life to attain the perfect shape.

I trained more than six hours daily in a gym, there I would find temporary and short-term relief. Little by little, the physical part started to withdraw and become depleted. That world started to be empty and destructive.

It was at that time that I began to suspect that I needed to devise other ways, because despite the perfection and beauty that I was seeing in my body, I felt betrayed and very hollow.

I was not the one I wanted for me. *I was for the others.* I sought myself so much outside that I neglected my internal needs. I never imagined that I would have so many seeds needing so much care. Water, light and a lot of love. My seeds were being lost to the passage of time. Crop after crop, fighting amongst themselves to transform into lush groves. My garden was at risk; my flowers were in danger of extinction.

Day after day, my colors were shrouded in shadow. My pretension of controlling everything, my arrogance and little care for self-respect jeopardized my four seasons. I lived in an eternal winter. The little warmth that I obtained was insufficient for everything that needed to flourish and explode within my own life.

Ceasing to wait for others and to diminish my love for myself became the most important battle in order to grow.

I alternated the physical exercise routine with pills and antidepressants, a thinness of soul and an excess of absences mingled with an infinite bitterness. For a while I had to take medicines. *Everything was very slow.* Every now and then they helped me seek passion and then, when things were going too fast, immediately I would take refuge in those chemical treats prescribed to slow the pace. In this way, my emotional *"yo-yo"* marked my life, leaving me powerless to quit the game.

In the succession of attempts, I will mention some that I tried for a while and that, surely, brought me into processes approximating "death" or should I say, "paths" … It was impossible not to go through it. From these experiences come a great deal of who I am and how I understand life as a human being. A high price, I should say.

For more than 20 years I strived to be constant with therapies or cures of the soul, both archaic and new. Psychoanalysis, Gestalt, Imago, Transpersonal Psychology, psychiatric or psychological help. It was a parade from any of the latest fashion catwalks. However, I didn't want to forsake all the things I was trying in parallel, even covertly: the legally institutional, and some that were not socially acceptable.

Meditations; spiritual retreats; reiki; metaphysics; fasting; therapy with mandalas; dance therapy; massages; martial arts; tobacco reading; sects; celibacy and devotion to the spiritual. Nevertheless, my luck didn't change as much as my expectations.

The therapies or cures started to take effect in due time. Or perhaps it was I in my own time. Things tried to transform within me, knowing that nothing had a solution unless "I" decided with perseverance, vision, enthusiasm and love what I wanted to *change* or, definitively, *to look at.* The cycles and repetitions were so obvious, that they were beginning to be the problem. I was exhausted, frustrated and possessed by rage. An ordinary addict. Lazy of the soul. Resentment or spiritual tourism were my constant reproach. The greatest spiritual merit is one's own life.

Finally, in that total emptiness, I tried drugs: the soft ones, the legal ones and the prohibited ones. I started with marijuana or cannabis, later a little cocaine combined with alcohol. However, my life continued to be deserted; not even this gave me a glimpse of light, at least, to benefit from. I realized that it didn't rely on anything or anybody. This began to develop into the deepest loneliness that I ever had to endure. There was nothing outside of me that would make me happier than to start walking my internal paths; those which, in the long run, proved to be the hardest, more difficult than any other process or experience that I had the opportunity to live.

Often times, I thought of madness as an alternative to quitting. Depression and sickness were stretching out their arms. My essence didn't give up. I kept wanting to search, to find myself. The search led me to encounter a soul full of shadows. *The path to healing is more like a constant movement than a happy ending.*

The emotions were the owners of the places that I could not activate. Asleep and with thousands of maladies, I would think incessantly. In short, there was no peace to guide me in any safe direction.

When the sadness was overwhelming, nothing contained light for me. I always thought that I came from a dysfunctional family and the most wonderful discovery was when I realized that it was so. I knew what the "Stockholm Syndrome"(1) was.

(1) The Stockholm syndrome is a psychological state in which the victim of a kidnapping, or a person detained against his own will, develops a relationship of complicity with his kidnapper. On occasion, the prisoner may end up helping the captor achieve their objectives.

Little by little, I plucked apart reality. I allowed myself to feel the terror in my body of being about to lose my life in the hands of the woman that gave it to me, *my own mother.*

Few emerge safely into life. Being born is a process as wonderful as it is complex. We bring and carry a task that is worthy of remembering, so that it doesn't turn against us on our path. When we are born, we all know what death means. In a silent way we carry it as a memory within each cell. It remains as a tattoo on each atom of the body. This is inevitable. Without being conscious, on many levels we know who receives the credit of that horrible experience. In this way we may spend a lifetime without confronting a truth called "fear of living."

Every story is always so subtle and, underneath, these wounds don't allow us to see our parents with trust. Especially toward "her," the giver of life, our Mother. We try to erase this experience, without noticing that minute after minute it is more tangible and irreparable. The stories and the pain not perceived with responsibility are the vehicles for the ghosts that we'll face along the path, again and again, until we can embrace and love them. See, acknowledge and love. From this comes the possibility of rewinding each second and turning it into something new. Otherwise, we are condemned to go around in a thousand circles until we can grasp some light.

I realized that by negotiating my survival as a child, I had to give up love. The boy or girl who learns how to love or that appears to do so, is the one that is controlled by the hands of its captors. The ones whom at any given time could terminate life itself. This does not mean the parents are "bad." *It is our body that helps us understand the care we must take to preserve life.*

Life sustains itself with this love, but only at times. It is our job to find the true meaning of what we all try to understand, about the overused word that has become the greatest enigma of all time:

Love.

The kids that are pampered to an extreme suffer all kinds of problems, even poor muscle tone. They end up hating their parents for not giving them the right to walk with strength. That energy is what hurts us and what makes us become great warriors. Everything transforms, no fate is incomplete.

Understanding this is what helped me recognize my mother as the perfect vehicle so that my vessel could land on the ground. I always searched for where her love was and many times I could find it … My heart decided to find it. Complaints, sadness and rage were winning the race against the woman who wanted to grow up to be responsible for her actions.

Growing up in a family where everything is negotiable, makes us awaken our intuition. Generally, the price can be quite high, because we are always great controllers and, due to mistrust, we live in a permanent state of barter. We do not dare to love, because we don't even know what the meaning of that word entails.

Sometimes, my own children would lose the joy of having me with them, by my insistence to seek pain that had no motive. Training is the key to the miracle.

I longed for perfection: to be flawless, tediously correct, accommodating. Once again, in this way my fear of not knowing how to live showed up. With all these mistakes I realized the only chance I had was to restructure my history, from my ancestors through to my cells, in order to be able to rejoice in the present. To always recognize the intention.

After accepting these stages as gifts—not as problems—my emotional life began to give way to something of which I had been completely unaware. This was my task and my commitment. Questioning myself and day by day, building a path, without holding my abductors responsible for my survival. Without a doubt, laziness is the misuse of creativity.

I started on my own to make internal movements with a lot of effort. This process transformed me from birth to being born again. It still continues with different nuances, such as the season of the year. While I narrate this part of my story, I still think upon the Mage and the man. These bottomless vessels filled with what I am certain could be a brew to savor myself better.

In the challenging years that I was forced to swim to the shores of my inner being, I experienced an episode that brought me back to life: I took the decision to love my mom, walk her path, swallow her into my soul, and understand that without her connection I would not get anywhere.

This process literally pulled off my skin and created another one. It meant disassembling the structure of those traumatic years, full of ideas, bribes, tantrums and all the hardest things that made my world transform, thanks to the internal alchemy, into a paradise full of responsibilities. It is the wounded child that seeks recognition from its wounds. In consequence, it disconnects from the reality of love and blames others for its failures. The way we accept our mother is the same way we go taking each day of our life. Each day I would wake up and find events within my story that had to do with being at risk and that no one was there for me. What to do? Well, as a practice, I adopted the habit of breathing, looking at the event and changing it within me. Just examining an event, without wishing to change anything about it, is a fire that, though it burns, comes to purify you. That small taste of having the strength to do it was already healing.

Thanks to this step, I started to love the woman that is within me, my menstruations, and the life that I had given to my kids. I began to love the man that took me as his woman to give me his children. To know myself as a mother, understanding the terror of putting life in danger in each act that brings life and more life. I searched for the names and stories of my great grandmothers and grandmothers: their frustrated loves, losses, poverty and injustices. All of this was only just beginning to be in order. Above all, myself.

By loving my parents, I was able to transform myself without cutting the lifeline. I understood that my task was to take our honest and wonderful legacy as human beings further. To find the place where doing what made me happy would be the highest challenge. During these years of such amazing processes, the Mage appeared like a butterfly, full of color and possibilities. She was a transcendental event in my life that allowed me to see what, without a doubt, I also needed to reveal.

The Mage guided me to research my soul and my origin. I understood the why and the how of the emotional torrents that shaped my own wounds.

Each emotion is connected to a thought. In turn, every thought is interconnected to a story. Healing the stories, seeing them from another angle—any angle—without trying to change them, without judging, manifested the possibility of setting off on new paths.

I began to see the big picture instead of the small one, to understand everything that effectively supported me.

In the end, I came to feel and understand the love and the struggles of my parents. Suicide, abandonment, slavery, prostitution, madness—to mention only some of the fates that mark people the most—framed the picture of those stories that now were exposed with more clarity in my life. To listen calmly and with respect made me realize that, in the end, I was only looking at my past, amplified, to be able to continue on the path. Stopping selfish behavior and seeing the time that was lost in the wrinkles around their eyes, full of mysteries and legends, left me with a lesson of humility that I had never experienced. Gradually I was able to restore an internal and harmonious order in my life, beginning to do something useful that I enjoyed. Each day, every day. A training for life.

From there I managed to reach an impartial place. I experimented with how my bones were growing quickly to emerge into a new life that would be full with challenge and truth.

The wounds became a mantle of stars. I still feel and breathe them; I make them mine. Now, I consider my temperament and my gratitude. Nothing is more beautiful than being able to look back and smile; the sensation now is that everyone supports me on my journey.

When it rains very hard, it doesn't matter where I am; I close my eyes and there I receive their applause from the earthly sky. The first step in detachment is love.

I'm still searching, but in another dimension. One of them is being with the Mage and transmitting her legacy, her enigma, that door which now appears to me as a gift for what I have accomplished on the path and in walking it. Especially in the passing of this last year, the Mage knew exactly what I had to do for homework in order to reach the place where I find myself now.

My little girl wounds; the teenager betrayed by not knowing the path of the soul; the belief that love is blind; to give it all to obtain and beg for affection; the female so thirsty for love, beyond what can be understood. The wise woman that wishes for the infinite understanding of what it is "to be."

Cobwebs delicately constructed to trap something that made me feel vitally trapped. The only certainty was that I should trust and believe in each moment, in order to enter into the Whole. Ceasing to see life through my wounds showed me a route that, until then, was unknown to me. Nothing changes until we change.

Everything was fertile ground to be sown.

To awaken has to do with ceasing to be ignorant in the face of life.

Mistrust and the absence of faith are the grandest paths we must walk to arrive at ourselves, God, One.

Surprisingly, the mechanism to escape any circumstance is fear. It becomes a silent motor. Everything is built around fear. Due to fear we have lost ourselves inside ignorance. The most fragile life and, by consequence, the most powerful one, is within our own fears.

"If I change, everything changes"

The clock advised me that the time of the encounter had arrived. The beautiful afternoon
made me feel blissful. My heart seemed like a whirlwind and my desire to be with the "man" was compelling. He would pick me up at six thirty, as agreed. From the main entrance of the old house where we were staying, home to the most beautiful flowers that I've ever seen, the view of the mountains and the sky could shake the cosmos of the Mage.

My outfit was suitable for a carnival of sensation: my baggy pants of many colors, an orange shirt, a shawl which had been given to me in the mystic, beautiful Guatemalan land called Tikal, where every knit in the fabric exhibited a blend of history and culture. The inspiration of its temples, walking trails, jungle and stele were invested in the essence of such lovely textiles.

In my decision to accept the meeting, and guarding my happiness at all costs, the word "guilt" showed up to give me a familiar fright. Intertwined with the girl, still insecure and in search of approval and acknowledgment, I chose to breathe and undertake the adventure with this one of the beautiful eyes, that made all my life worth it.

I looked at the clock again and realized that the scheduled time had already passed, by a few minutes. This hour would not return again.

I then thought of the present moment and its alternatives.

The old demons constructed by my mind started to wander. I decided not to feed them to stay in the truth of the present moment that was passing by.

By not deceiving myself and being able to confront the truth, I knew that my only fear was the chance of running into the Mage and having to give her an explanation. Each second was terrifying because of this possibility.

I confronted myself saying, "There is nothing to hide. You are not doing anything wrong." The Stockholm syndrome was up to its old ways from the unforgettable past. However, this time there were no abductors present in my life.

I was the only one to face my responsibility, so I stood with the appearance of a confident woman and continued waiting for my star bearer.

For a few minutes I walked around the old house. I looked attentively at each well-arranged detail that, in essence, made it a very special place, energetically. Candles that were lit day and night were placed on each step or stone shelf inside and outside of the house. The containers of drinking water for the guests had some sort of cap made of crystal that allowed light into the precious liquid. The sculptures were simple stones, ordered by size that possessed the perfect balance to support each other.

Fountains full of running water produced a very natural melodic symphony. Hanging dreamcatchers adorned each corner, making the spiders feel content with their home.

I walked with a rhythmic step and closed my eyes to see internally, enjoying the wonder of starting over and envisioning the external as a manifestation of what I desired the most. *I'm changing and I no longer hold onto the past.*

I savor only the trembling of my legs and the scent of my soul.

Internally, a woman filled with colors and journeys. I began to comprehend the word destiny and the enthusiasm to live it. I was alert, awake. Now no one could take away the sensation of stepping with my heart.

I started to go down the small hill from where you could see the house. Once again, the lovely landscape reminded me a thousand times of the exact moment when the soul yearns to give itself the opportunity to change, akin to spring.

A little garden served as an ornament beside a pond replete with fish. Watching them, I wondered: "How can they survive winter and frozen water?" I imagined how it would be to exist there, without thinking of anything, simply waiting for a change in order to carry on living.

I got carried away by thousands of unanswered questions. They were only fish, nothing else.

They would wait for the change of season to be able to nourish the water with life. As I moved forward, enjoying the walk alone, I observed the blue of the sky closely. Along the way I came across a tree full of apples. I took two. One for me and one for my little girl.

I like the idea of giving gifts to my inner little girl once in a while. This girl goes for a walk every time we both desire. We have fun many times making pranks. She likes ice cream and I let her dance until she is exhausted.

This way, keeping her calm, the adult woman takes care of the important matters and neither of us interferes with the other. It is my responsibility to hug her so she discovers the true path of love, preventing her from feeling fear when there is no affection. She nourishes the home of the grown up that little by little has built its home. From here we begin in the understanding that, in the quest for a savior, we encounter the healers that we are: ourselves. When I was able to see my life with happiness, gratitude and respect, everyone—surprisingly—made me very happy.

I was lost in time, and was starting to feel the cold on my face. Yet, my heart was still warm, full of seasons, each one willing to make space for the next one. Everything in due time. I looked up and saw an immense field of maize a few meters from the road. The idea of turning it into a hideout, where I might find my own desires, enchanted me. I rushed to touch it and observe it. I walked and entered into this field full of fertile stalks for a while. All the earth is full of miracles. As I looked ever closely at the maize I had new and exciting sensations. I had never before walked into a postcard.

The shape and arrangement of each small grain, protected by the corn silk of its leaves, the order, the perfect sequence. Thousands of them surrounded me. Everything made me realize that heaven was on earth. The greatest manifestation was lost by not being awake.

Maybe the only thing that was happening to me was that I had started to be alive, and in some way so conscious that finally everything around me stopped being ordinary—each thing was magic before my eyes—To the extent that my walk became a journey with no return. Suddenly I felt I was in a labyrinth improvised by the land and, although I was enjoying it with serenity, I wondered: "Who will know where am I now?" I imagined my loved ones: "What were they doing now?"

I closed my eyes. I hugged myself fervently to the plants, keepers of the fruit, to feel the capacity to expand my desire for love, to my people. The intention was enough. I let them know that I was where I wanted to be. I knew that that peace was sufficient to quiet the thoughts and stories that always repeat themselves to torture us. We are one from the beginning of knowing that we are together and connected.

Hence, the journey would fill up with cosmic and infinite connections. I felt so happy that I was able to surprise myself in a strange and unfamiliar space; I had to trust. If I was joyful, others would be as well … or maybe not. I had to be okay with this as well. I looked again at the maize field and remembered the *Popol Vuh* and the dishes that adorned the culinary history of the American Indians. I felt the hand of the farmer and the magic of planting, and then harvesting. The wisdom of the woman, connoisseur of the seeds, symbol of fertility in the land; giver of life.

That afternoon, with so much walking, sun, and gifts, brought understanding of something basic and powerful: no seed has an end. Life always brings more life through it.

With this feeling, deep and simple at the same time, I began to come out of that universal labyrinth that had unconsciously invited me to enter the forces of life and its true paths. I sent blessings to my seeds: my children and the people that helped me to grow (despite my pain), to each person that I had hurt without even knowing. Careless with myself, blindness had been my tool of growth for a long time.

Inside those wonderful images, one in particular came to mind: I wanted to be a warm cob, dipped in butter, ready to be devoured by that hungry man that was waiting for me. The mere possibility that he would thresh my body little by little made the time pass more slowly.

"Seeking the crossroad"

At a distance, on the hill, I could discern the sound of a small motorcycle. It was approaching down the road leading to the house we were staying in. Bit by bit the postcard began to widen. When it stopped in front of me, I knew that the evening had suddenly started when I realized that this was the knight that I had been waiting for. He looked like a modern day Quixote. He was quite a character, as if plucked from a comic strip and, even so, I was excited to be included in that tale. I couldn't hold my laughter. He also gave me his smile as if he was a newly awakened sun, and without a word between us, he invited me to get on his motorized horse and we left. To travel hugging his body felt like a blessing to me. I felt an air of freedom, whilst the scenery opened up unexpected endless possibilities to us.

I closed my eyes and could feel the nuances of life in the chilly wind that caressed my cheeks. "How could you put all of this together?" I wondered. I smiled with the Universe that once again was presenting a new road behind such a simple door, and which was, at the same time, blessed.

I experienced the light of the dusk as something unique. "The violet hour," as the Mage would call it, where everything transmutes, the mountains, the solitude of the earth full of expansive nourishment. I felt sacred. I raised a prayer to the sky above and said:

"Thank you, mother!"

This was the true portal to the Universe. I myself was the Key; had been searching for the way to the door. The tears ran down my face uncontrollably, but this time they were different; I could enjoy and savor them as if they were a delicacy. I felt my body, on earth and for the first time, ready to enter into true spirituality.

I couldn't stop thinking of the Mage; I was grateful for her having shown me the path. I was with her and this meant that the same magic would envelop it all and forever. I felt a great appreciation for all the roads that at some point I had taken, for the people that had accompanied me, and especially, for that which never worked out, since it kept me always searching.

Out of nowhere and in the midst of the short drive on my great adventure with my knight, everything completed inside of me and made sense. *I should just give thanks to the Whole.*

The pleasure of the breeze made me realize the state of communion I was in; I felt closely merged with the Word. Along the route, of just a few miles, my body—clinging to his body—would let itself soar in its desire to embrace him. Without expectations, plans or agreements, I promised myself only to have a good time.

To live only the present, the blessed moment that was in front of me: no more *past* nor *future*.

When a path is built on truth, it is made between a hello and a goodbye.

That space, with awareness, is the most wonderful that exists when its discovery is imminent, because it allows us to get away from the wounds and the abandonment, and prevents us from placing an extra burden on the dreams and expectations that we have; those which, generally, are never fulfilled.

Finally we arrived at our destination. The cold was permeating my very soul. My nose was freezing, in complete contrast to the rest of my skin. None of what I was wearing was appropriate for the season, let alone for a motorcycle ride. However, I was able to cheer myself without much complaint and disguise the cold that was consuming me. That man was looking at me with a moving tenderness. I knew that my smile came from acknowledging the truth. I was frozen and numb.

A typical Swiss house, with its carved roof in the shapes of waves, was the first of what I could observe. Facing this you could see the barn with its machinery, still warm after finishing a workday. It was quite an experience to observe the animals, especially the immense cows with their cowbells, whose sounds seemed like *echoes* from the past. You could still spot the sun that intended to set in the horizon, knowing that at any moment it would yield its space to the night and what hid within it.

He took me by the hand and helped me with the shawl. He guided me to the entrance of the house.

Ahead of the door to the anteroom was an old pond where animals drank water, and it had been transformed into a decorative object; now it was a wishing well. The sound of its drops, which made ripples on its surface, left me completely hypnotized and perplexed. They were like divine portals that were about to be breached.

Kindly, he opened the door and tactfully invited me to take off my shoes. After he did the same with his shoes, my gaze was briefly entertained with observing how and with what care he aligned my shoes next to his.

Afterward he stared at me and shared enthusiastically:

"There are two doors and one path. Which one would you like to take?"

Never before have I received such an enigmatic and tempting proposal. This made my doubts and my fear of making a mistake once again come to my awareness. I closed my eyes. With a subtle voice I said: "The one on the right."

My knight smiled as if my choice was the answer he had been waiting for. I wondered what was behind the door on the left. Immediately, he whispered in my ear, "I did not expect any less of you."

Then I told myself, "Let's continue."

The door opened slightly. Slowly I was transported to the text of *One Thousand and One Nights*. The scent of myrrh transported me to an infinity I knew was in my soul and acted like a balm. An aroma that was all innuendo. *Perfume or medicine? Sensual aroma or drug? Myrrh.*

My body sensed the *passages* filled with that aroma. Willingly I took pleasure from the air and its spell.

The music that bounced in the air evoked a Rumi poem with its dance on the earth synchronized with the cosmos and its fervent dervishes. Dancing candles.

Cushions made with the finest silks and carpets that sparked your imagination foreshadowed the flight into another dimension.

Here you could have written stories of love or adultery, or simply narrated novels of chivalry and tales of crimes of passion. One scene after another, where my mirage was conjoined with the aroma, and the woman. I closed my eyes and was able to feel the presence of *Scheherazade*, the one who captivated everyone with her stories in order to cling to life. The bed materialized in one corner, and then the place resembled a palace, a kind of Arab tent where the thousand myths of the Arabian Nights would be reedited to make an updated version of that timeless book that would continue writing itself with my experiences.

I tried to adapt myself to the situation to avoid showing my expression of surprise and fascination.

He asked me to make myself comfortable in any place in the living room. I looked around the space until I placed myself at a table that was at ground level. The sacred had been expressed in the form of delicacies: dates, fruits, pine nuts and cookies for guests, with infinite spices all new to my sense of smell and taste. Two cups sat unattended, waiting for tea. Its aroma invoked the Middle East. Suddenly, I imagined that their vapors rose to whisper the mysteries of the invisible in my ear. The magic in the union of two people.

For an instant I was alone. He said:

"You are in your temple, make yourself comfortable." I felt free once again to continue surveying the space. The waiting lasted a few minutes.

Sounds coming from the kitchen made me aware that something was being put in order. I rose from the floor to walk to an elongated table behind a wall. It wasn't easy to spot. There I stopped and realized that it was not a table, but a sacred altar. I was speechless, paralyzed by the spiritual world that was before me. During the tiresome years of searching, I clung onto so many things that, little by little, I dismissed everything till I was left with nothing. It seemed like what I had thrown in the trash at that time, had returned once again in front of my eyes. A postponed faith appeared in a variety of beliefs, energies, religions and sensations that I couldn't define.

For a second I thought that I had fallen into a trap. I was feeling so bad that I almost fainted. I remembered my rage and how I had ceased to believe in everything since nothing had worked for me. The music continued making me dizzy with the dancing of the candlelight. The aroma of the incense reminded me that it was a symbol of honor and respect toward the gods, but also part of the ritual in sacrifices. The millennial dates also took me away from the present moment. I had to rub my eyes and keep calm; this setback was so real, that I feared that the magic and illusion would vanish before my eyes.

Quartz, feathers and flowers surrounded the image of the teacher Jesus, his legacy and what is evident in the path of love. The presence of Siddhartha Gautama, the Buddha; the wonder of achieving attentive observation and the total equanimity of human consciousness through his own consciousness. Observing himself, he came to know himself. The Mother Tara, the *feminine Buddha* of wisdom and active compassion. Shiva Kriya, to whom was granted the highest instruction for mankind to fulfill its purpose, to reach the cosmic consciousness. A beautiful effigy of the beloved Kwan Yin, Goddess of mercy and love, capable of bringing the flame of comprehension and compassion from the very heart of God.

Krishna, who was born in a prison; the teachings of how God has to incarnate and appear in the dark and narrow prison house of our hearts so that we can obtain light and win freedom. *Ah, the eyes were burning and the heart was opening.*

Lakshmi, worshiped in India as the Goddess of wealth and beauty. It is believed that those who adore her know immediate happiness. Usually she is depicted with her partner Vishnu, the conqueror of darkness. As a sacred expression of all the forms of prosperity, she is perhaps the most popular of all the Hindu gods and goddesses.

Finally, there was the image of the great teacher Ramana Maharshi, an important figure in Hindu religion, one of the best known of the twentieth century. He belonged to the *adwaita vedanta* doctrine (there are no souls and God, but rather the souls are God). The core of his teachings was the atma- vichara, the inquiry of the soul.

This image in particular struck me like a bolt of lightning. It was like a time machine with its causalities. Just recently I had attended a retreat in Costa Rica. His photo was placed between books, positioned in such a way that his presence would be understood as something important. I looked at it every time I could. Each morning and every instant that I was in silence I would get lost in his eyes and I would like the sensation of connecting with the strength of his great, calm and humble energy.

I never knew who he was; what mattered was what my heart told me in those moments. Then I started to inquire about his existence and discovered this passage, which has stayed with me ever since: "Why do you occupy yourself with gods that come and go? Haven't you noticed that the mantras, rituals and prayers are excellent only to a certain degree? There comes a time when you have to abandon all of that. Only when you have left everything behind, including the gods, do you achieve vision without beginning or end, the vision of the Supreme Being."

Well, here were almost all of the images that pertained to my struggle—on an altar in the home of a stranger; it seemed like a spy was uncovering my past. Where was I? Who was this man? Was the Mage involved in all that I was witnessing?

I went back to the cushions; lay my soul against the wall, dazed. The wild wavy hair appeared with the steaming water for the herbs, kisses from the earth. We stayed in an uncomfortable silence. I couldn't do much; I could only give in to the hidden desires of all my lives. That sacred place full of enigmas was welcoming me, and this man could speak the essence without saying a word; his eyes were imprinted on my life.

In that space of silence there was no room for any question. Any inappropriate comment would have ended that wonderful connection. It was impossible to put into words. In a second, the space became narrower. Time was made complete with these two people that shared paths and skies. They were two spirits that understood each other in such a way, that with only one look they felt inseparable. Past lives that were, perhaps, hiding in the light of the dancing candles, in some dates and a Rumi that was still waiting for his Shams of Tabriz.

From time to time, I looked at his long wavy hair illuminated by the light, his dark skin tanned by the sun of the deserts. He was like an oasis to the sight of anyone thirsty for love. At any moment I could capsize in his harbor. His lips were an ocean in the midst of a tempest and I was afraid of losing my vessel in that storm. Suddenly, the roof overhead opened with a view to the sky, the candles started to flicker and time vanished. The images seemed to come to life and I could only bow my head. With a voice as sweet as honey, he told me, "My heart is your home."

He covered me with a silver blanket printed with stars. I was telling stories to my soul to be able to survive. Rumi and Shams climbed to the roof with me. I closed my eyes and lay my head down.

I didn't know from where, but the Word was of God. I knew of the divine presence through my work; the labor that one does with so much fervor and respect. I also knew that the door to God was the parents and the path to God was the partner: the opposites, the completeness and the mirrors.

The Mage and her teachings … It was impossible not to remember her at that moment amidst the stars. The music, the veils, the altars, the stars and the beloved, now taking me by the hand and rocking me like waves in the sea. I lost myself. I surrendered myself, and then I knew what it was to use my own magic. The sensations of love, protection and the spiral of life joined and I felt calmed by the blessed rocking motion of his long arms, looking only to soothe my bones and my mind.

I erased time, and transformed into presence. Waves of new sensations washed over me. I tried not to be overwhelmed. I wanted to allow myself to be dazzled at the wonder of being a woman. To be so present, abandoning the stories, gave me the sensation of experimenting with a different peace next to my beloved. Soon I would open the portals and would know the union at another level.

I didn't want to question myself about the true spirituality; I knew of God's dwelling on earth. The space that He inhabits between a woman and a man. It was time to offer up the mysteries of the skin. I devoted myself to silence and I felt my body preparing to reach the absolute, outside of itself. I started to know his home, that he assured me was my heart. We shared tea at times from the same cup. I wanted to take a pause and ask him the content of such a splendid brew. He denied this by shaking his head, at the impossible idea of revealing the contents of a millennial secret. I insisted with curiosity. Then he complied, sharing the coveted secret, which I had to keep.

"The content of the tea is based on some ingredients brought directly from Arab countries," he explained. "When women are ready to give birth and succeed in giving life, this miraculous delicacy is presented to the ones that visit the new member of the family. Prepared by the wise and elder women, everyone shares it, sipping to celebrate the recent childbirth. I cannot reveal its ingredients precisely," he proclaimed, "since the one we are drinking at this moment was a gift from my own grandmother. She is capable of curing souls just with this brew. However, I can assure you it contains nutmeg, cinnamon, ginger, anisette, sweet clover and some others that I don't remember."

Then he added, "The most important secret ingredient are pieces of the tree of life; the only one which manages to live in the desert and resist the harshness of nature and time." The story transported me. I yearned to meet the wise woman with magical hands. I closed my eyes and thanked her, enjoying the evening and its secrets. It had all the requirements to call it the ritual of life.

Love was imminent, just and deserving. We exchanged the dates while stories and ancestral tales crossed our lips. The sweetness and tenderness were so erotic that it was impossible not to feel that the ambience, layers of aromas, and the tent full of cushions were expecting our encounter. I can close my eyes and relive it all. I can relive it in this moment, the night gets into my skin and the aromas take me away ...

I let his breath caress me. There was nothing in the dim candlelight that his eyes could not see, thirsting for my essence.

Very carefully he removed the veils from a door that scarcely revealed the entrance, transporting us to Him. I let myself be carried in his arms.

Lying down in the tent of the Arabian Nights, he slid his hand through the blanket of stars and kissed me. Then he made a very sensitive pause for my soul and said to me, "Rest in your home. I'll wait for your heart."

Can one become intoxicated with the cosmos? Feel the *divine* of eternity? Resting in the nectar of his presence, I guided him with my hands and my lips to each hidden corner that ought to be explored by skin other than mine. The music, the incense and the tree of life were the witnesses of what we were allowing to happen. The sounds reverberated in the walls of the temple and made echoes through the candlelight.

I wanted to erase space and time and let myself be carried away. At times the weariness of the soul would wake me and there he was, looking at me and licking me with all of his heart. His eyes told me that he wanted every last bit of what I was willing to offer.

Dreams and stories assaulted me, knocking on my door with the intent to return me to the pit of my past. I knew that this man could not crumble over my doubts or my past. He was only waiting to be invited to feel one with God. It was a night of spiritual respite and this allowed us to embrace the fury of the skin. We merged. Pleasure made us invoke the sacred word: *union*. Word made reality when there was an alliance of the whole with the whole.

I'm all wet and have a fire that he is now searching within…

Ninth Path

"The darkness of the light"

Day broke. The soft light of the sun barely covered our bodies, full with pleasure, merged in the joy of their plenitude. We were not the same. The night had worked its magic and we were no exception.

He wrapped me with his arms of light that were gleaming in my eyes. He moved closer, bringing a sip of hot tea to my mouth. I drank the love from this magical brew. Meanwhile he said: "The water for your bath is ready."

What a delightful path I had taken; at least until that moment, it felt like the road to the sun, without any risk that my wings would melt. However, at every moment one has to educate oneself. The more we open up to the possibility of claiming victory, the more we should become aware of the opportunity to learn and experience, and be humble while the lessons of life and what we need to learn from them transpire. From this place, we can know power and its depths.

I knew that I had always been a special woman, but seeing myself in everything that I always knew I deserved made me feel strange.

He took my hand and helped me up, and we left the tent of Arabian Nights, that still kept the sheets warm. Everything had that aroma.

Upon entering the bathroom, I was baffled to see the bathtub filled with steaming water. The fragrance it released made me linger with the sensuality of the night that had escorted us to the sunrise. Colorful rose petals were floating in the water like an artist's palette.

It was not a dream. It was real. Here was the guardian of my soul and my body; he had dedicated his time and energy to avail himself of nature and resources.

He helped me immerse slowly in the lukewarm water. Flow, liquid, the essence. Once there, when I felt relaxed and totally calm, I closed my eyes and let my vessel float. The sultan of ancient times came closer, little by little. After a subtle, wet and slow kiss, he said: "I would like to show you the marks that created the path of my life; I want you to see them in the light."

I held myself back. I was surprised and puzzled by this request. I couldn't move, much less blink.

He took off his white cloth robe and let it fall to the floor. This revealed the scars that obscured sixty percent of his skin. The entire right side was carved by the marks of fire and its intense heat, having burned the skin extensively. It exhibited an unusual color, melted, wrinkled, and creased; forever engraved by the flames. I began to reflect myself in him as if his wounds were mine.

Staring at him, I knew I was looking at my own body, the one I had rejected so many times. Any reason or motive for that was absurd. I remained silent.

I didn't want to intervene in that moment with any sort of peculiar comment or question. In spite of what we were experiencing, it was difficult not to feel compassion and a little pity for my storybook knight.

There was no space for anything. In absolute silence I scanned each detail of the map of his physique. I didn't dare to speak a word. He looked at me and understood my reticence.

Next came the lesson that would culminate in shaking my path.

He approached the tub, and close to me, with much tenderness he said, "I like the love with which you manage to see me. I hope that one day you feel the same compassion for yourself."

Silence was my enemy.

The comment from my kind man with his armor ended up crushing me without mercy.

He stood up, retrieved the white cloth robe from the floor and, once his soul was covered, he prepared to leave the confines of the bathroom. A wound was starting to open that seemed eternal. I couldn't place the thing that had resulted in splitting me in two. I was astonished for a while. However, my thoughts and reflections were not coming from the exterior. My tears were the familiar thorns of the roses that I had always tried to avoid.

It was true: I felt compassion for everyone else, but not with myself. What had just happened was the beginning of a lesson. The capacity to give so much love to others always left me with charred skin and heart. There could not be an honest love that didn't start with me. I felt strange in a world that I didn't know well. Becoming aware, to cease being dumb was the lesson that I had to practice with prudence. Everything new, or all over again to do it differently?

Long minutes went by, sitting in the tub, the petals speaking to me with their silent beauty. I started to get up and reach for the towel hanging on the wall near the tub. I looked in the mirror at the image of my face. I observed myself for a long time; I saw visages that changed over and over. Was it me? How many of us were in the illusion of reality? I was careful and kind to scan it and admire each detail that I had rejected before. I was grateful to my skin, my legs and everything that my hands were able to reach. I left the bathroom and, staring into his eyes, I felt that we both had affection in our being. We embraced each other in silence for a long time. We rejoiced in the space, and in respect.

The knight with a considerate sword would be waiting for me until I was ready to return. There was complicity in our gaze. Each hand found its opposite by means of the gratitude and honesty of us both. He looked at me with the same compassion that I had lacked and never given myself. In reality the love that you are unaware of is more harmful than the pain of habitual indifference.

I walked to the door and once again I was balanced like life itself; I felt everything in the right flow; everything had merged with me and I felt that I was molding myself with all of it.

Now I had to advance to the *next step*; always to decide what should remain, continue or *end*.

Back at the antiquated house, the fog was still honoring the landscape. The morning dew prevented the light from rising in the mountains, which graced the new day. Serenity, tranquility, and enjoyment adorned the path for both of us.

What was it that was changing? How was it that everything changes? Questions and more questions. I stopped myself and said: "If something is changing, I do not need to know what it is or how, only that it has changed."

I felt closer to my life and its vessel, and a purpose that appeared as a wake-up call.

To abide with the experience of what had been lived would lead me to know myself more. Confronting the other made me know myself in the darkest place, but this blessed peace made me feel full, regarding life and my quest.

That which was essential was already happening within and without me. I began to appreciate the difference between the tempestuous loves compared to the subtle ones and the less passionate ones. I started to commemorate the man who had marked my soul and skin for so many years.

Everything passed by very fast while we made our way to the house. It was inevitable to review the balance and commence an internal audit of the profits and the losses. Were there ever losses?

Then, the word "love" began to march before my eyes to perceive its real meaning. It was impossible not to recount the same story, which I would repeat to myself many times till boredom. Once again, as time passed by and we reached the house, I got lost in thoughts of the past and what was … why not say it? Healed.

The man, my companion of the journey. The "inscribed soul," as I like to call him.

When we met, each one of us was carrying our divorces, breakups, abandonments, deceptions and … *stop counting*.

A couple of kids on each side and the hope to build a family that we longed for with all of our heart.

We caressed our skin and our souls by celebrating with a sizzling hot night. The host of that event was nothing more and nothing less than *destiny*, something that was impossible to predict. However, when love drags you by the hair, it leaves you no options and there is nothing else to do but surrender to that fact. The essential voids make their appearance and we pretend, desperately, to fill them from the outside. Nevertheless, there is nothing more impossible than to deny life its flow and its teachings; this is the only thing I was able to experience and continue living from this love. The idea of staying in passion has to do with the capacity of discovering ourselves daily with the other.

The "inscribed soul" had hair as white as the love that everyone woman wants to have in a state of purity. We had undertaken a life uncovered; the greatest revelation and transformation that I had lived as a woman, at least until that time.

Blindly in love, full of vacancies and with desires of perfection, I began to realize that this love was full of few valid things.

It came to be repetitive story of what was learned at a distance, things from home, the daily routine of the child that grew up making emotional blackmail to survive again and again.

The life and time which we exerted ourselves to build, could only be accomplished through the unlimited pleasures of the skin, devoid of soul. Sex, sex, and sex. We obliged ourselves to believe that one should love the other at any cost. We both insisted in perfection that neither understood. We neglected the truth, which is inside each one of us, to avoid going through that which was necessary within our relationship. Crippled in everything, we began to crawl, confusing ourselves with the risk of falling further and further down. This way we came to look in each other's eyes every now and then. After the euphoria, the insults, the violence and the lack of respect, we ended up making love again to take from the skin what might be lost at any moment. Upon finishing the emotional barbarity, we looked at each other so lost and hurt, that we lamented everything, in the madness of forgiveness adapted to blame. We became useless and yet we called this "the greatest love on earth."

Our activities, jobs, and relationships with the family and friends entered a stage of danger. Nothing had meaning any longer and rage was the companion to both of us.

We proceeded to isolate ourselves slowly with the excuse of protecting our fears. Everything started to constrict and become very narrow. The suffering of a relationship full of mistrust and insecurity ended by taking control of our journey. I was always a woman inclined to be unfaithful, disloyal and complaintive. The questions were always, Where is that which will make me happy? What would make me happy? I knew that no man who would share his life with me would be enough. I was never loyal to the commitment that a relationship meant. This way, I ensured the distance that prevented me from knowing love and its paths. Being a traitor was a good excuse to know myself as an invalid in every way. What I least tolerated about myself were two things: the first, seeing myself uncovered over and over in that which I wanted to do, and second, seeing myself as a victim of my own actions. I would jump between searching and blaming. This was the foundation of my exploration each time I searched for the love that was not yet within me.

Women are not monogamous and men know it. Our inner strength is so wonderful and powerful that, before using it to its fullest, we *convince* ourselves that we are victims of everything that happens around us, including the matters of the heart. We like a man of power and they are fascinated by a woman with self-knowledge, wisdom, direction, and most of all, very feminine qualities. However, by living in that permanent emptiness, we don't know how to appreciate the difference between loving completely or being free; we prefer to make our men responsible for the misfortune that we have procured ourselves for our entire life. It fills us with pleasure to see how one man confronts another for territory and for his female. We consider it a sensual and seductive act. We like them to make love to us—if we have to fake an orgasm; we do it. We are left completely empty of soul, but we make the man believe that he has made us very happy; when in truth, what we want is the male's semen, to make him our property so that no other female can have him.

It is preferable to wear him out so that, even if he goes to another woman, he arrives debilitated.

I meditate in depth; I visit my grandmothers in other planes of existence. Powerful women, beautiful and fertile. I like to feel that they were great seductresses and desired women. I never believed that it was all about knitting in a rocking chair, while watching the sunset with the eyes of a lamb.

Every woman has a marvelous power.

Truly intelligent women never quit love in any of its forms.

We have two hearts, the feminine and the masculine. Having this energy integrated connects us with our inner power and, even in war, calms the most fierce man. Man seeks external wars because he ignores the inner ones.

The woman calms the external wars, since she knows of the inner ones. To possess knowledge of the heart prevents the spirit from running dry. Women learn what life wants, understanding the fertile soil and its seeds. They deny the search for power by using their children to obtain beauty and eternal youth. The woman that knows how to be a woman abandons the role of the witch in the quest for power, and transforms into a Mage because she knows her power. The mages are capable of loving all women, young and old. They have to experience a transformation of knowledge in order to understand that there are certain powers that can revert back to harm them. From this point occur the major transformation and the path toward the Mage.

Additionally, I had wanted to be the perfect woman in that unhappy relationship. I wanted to attempt the path of being the devoted and self-sacrificing woman that I could never be.

In those days, I went back a thousand times to play the same wounded and accommodating girl with the man that I believed I loved. In each renewed phase, I liked to test the formula of the unknown, even though luck was not on my side by resisting the right thing to do. I had already been hurt long enough, and this time I intended to give my heart to the point where I could again become like a rag, as long as I could maintain my relationship. Those stubborn loves that never die, because we prefer to suffer. I must admit that the injuries that I inflicted on various occasions didn't make me a saint.

I began to merge myself once again with the Stockholm syndrome. "Thank God, there is a definition for the relationship that some of us develop with ourselves and our so called 'beloved.' The union is based on a slow detriment, but is very secure."

It is demanding and difficult to understand that this type of dependency is not a reason to grow together. Abusive, controlling, capable of violating your soul, it represents neither passion nor love. It is just insanity.

We started to separate in stages. Intermittence became routine in our lives. Each month, each week, the relationship accumulated more unhappiness. The emotional exhaustion for us both and, in consequence, for our loved ones, our children, who witnessed our chaotic conduct spinning in circles, was unsustainable. Despite this, new formulas for disrespect appeared, with a growing mistrust that started to transform it all into something very dangerous. Likewise, I thought this was love and that at any moment our lives could change. I still believed in something miraculous, the irresponsibility of asking that something be resolved, while I repudiated myself for the inertia and lack of decision.

"I hate you" was heard more often than any other enthusiastic expression, and this way the daily repertoire was filled with aggression and abuse. We couldn't communicate, much less love. Jealousy and mutual competition brought us close to self-destruction. Many times I thought of erasing him and something in me would say, "You are exactly like him." The continuous crises and errors were interminable.

Then I began to feel exhaustion akin to losing the desire to live; to feel terror that he would ambush me with *anything* that might make me appear "unreliable," or that I could not prove. I stopped taking care of my basic needs and of my own life.

I preferred that my phone would not ring. I began to shut myself inside of me; I abandoned my work until little by little, inevitably, I imprisoned myself in my own story. Like so many women, what I had done was invent an asylum in which to confine myself, and yet be able to say that *I loved intensely.*

The relationship had too long been hanging by a thread; it ended up breaking at the thinnest part. During the breakup process, in the emotional sway that we had established, we sought professional help, but we never knew how to accept it. Sadly, we arrived at the conclusion that we could not exist without pain. We were addicted to this terrible phenomenon called *suffering*, a kind of narcotic that makes you feel alive, without ever letting you know what life is all about.

All we did for one another was remind ourselves, consistently, of the ability to endure a life in perpetual collapse. This way, we arrived at the fact that, in each goodbye, there was the possibility that someone else would come in and rescue us from what we were living through, as did happen in the end. After a prudent time of silence and distance, each of us was able to sustain their life in other simultaneous relationships, withholding the rage and grief of knowing we had been unsuccessful in trying to grow and keeping what we had both desired.

When the relationship failed from one side or the other, we would again ride the ups and downs of madness. Nothing seemed to end. Returning for another attempt, the last one, I decided to undertake a direction that would finally remove me from the hole that I had dug for myself.

Knowing how painful what I had to do would be, I made the decision to ask him that we try one more time; but this time the difference would be in being very conscious of my needs. I only wanted to be authentic with myself, though the mere possibility of being happy and spontaneous in front of him continued generating terror within me.

I realized that I had panicked about being lonely, even while being with him. This was the first step in recognizing what I wanted from a partner, when my loneliness had no end.

I recognized the depths of my own jealousy filled with a volatile neurosis. My own insecurity and mistrust destroyed my desire for company, or that, which might be called a "relationship."

However, at the same time as I write this, despite the pain that it may have caused, I must admit that it has been one of the best experiences of the journey. The feeling that a torrent of flooding water opened new channels so that everything possible would flow. Pain was not an option in love, but I had to feel it to learn that. Suffering is not necessary, we have to abandon it, considering that it doesn't lead us anywhere. I learned that I was able to remain indefinitely in a love, knowing that it was dysfunctional. For a good part of my life I chose the options of war, cruelty, disrespect and violence as if all of these things were proof of love. Now I know it's not like this, and it can be different.

I remember those days and I have no alternative than to say, "Thank you." A feeling of deep and renewing relief. Our lives were on the verge of madness. It is good to revise the story as often as necessary, to experience it without tantrums; to allow whatever manifested to flourish within. In recognizing what it was, how it was, we undertake the greatest act of responsibility with our lives, and this must prevail over any pain, since only by going through it can we feel relief, and most of all, avoid retracing the same steps. To fight or deny it, on the contrary, is the perfect formula to continue tying us more and more to pain. It has the effect of an invisible elastic band; the more you push, the more bound you remain. It's the typical "I hate you, don't leave me."

Each time that, from the heart, I examine this part of my story, I see myself in time as the girl that wanted—but didn't know how—to grow and learn. The greatest task now is to love and transform myself with respect and dignity, with perseverance and enthusiasm, and a permanent focus on that which I desire. Many things helped me understand the reasons I found myself a love like that, but whatever they might be, I will always have my heart open to know that I was also responsible for what happened. That's the only thing that guarantees me to have and to keep a grateful heart.

When I visit any city and I sit in the park where kids are distracting themselves playing, I imagine that we both remained there forever, struggling for a toy or eternally awaiting the yearned recognition for any deed.

Now the adult and mature woman can see them at a distance and occasionally, if I wish, I bring them candies and try to hug them so they don't need to continue surviving amid so much war.

To the men that I was able to love and to the ones that I could not love in return, today I thank them for so many stories that I lived, even those that I still don't comprehend and continue to make paths with. When I remember them I love them all deeply, just as they are, as they were in their essence, whatever that is. Each one, in the way they were able to, led me to know myself more, to becoming the one I am today.

Wherever they are and especially to you, thank you for every day that we shared. To the ones I don't recall and may have hurt, I say,

—I'm sorry for what happened.

As adults, we are now responsible and each of us can take alternate routes, different from the fight and the devastation.

"Energy moves thanks to energy"

I learned from the Mage about the consequences which operate exactly the same, whether two persons are connected by the bond of love, or the contrary. Generating good thoughts toward others was not a new thing to me. However, being able to understand the energy, feeling it in its true space and dimension, has been one of the things that has made me more cautious and, above all, respectful. No one deceives destiny, much less another person.

Energy comes to be understood under the word "love"; we cannot believe, and it is impossible to pretend, that we could capture it for our own use. By the act of simply opening the windows of the soul, the universal interconnections take care of putting everything in perfect synchronicity.

Faced with this demonstration of an atomic bomb, we must abandon the space for the complaints department; it no longer exists. It is meaningless to say, "Give me back the kisses that I gave you." When it is time for us to live it, it manifests.

One of the greatest lessons of the Mage had to do with the power of energy. I had barely got into the knowledge and transmission of it, when I realized that the majority of things do not have an explanation. The understanding of the scientific aspects often remain in doubt, even as new quests corroborate that which is always discovered. The awakening of consciousness, more than energy itself, is a science with little foundation on earth. Everyone has to live what comes their way, and faced with this, there is no possible explanation.

In South America there is an indigenous population whose conflicts are resolved in a manner that can be very strange for us. When there is war between communities, the warriors must await the fate of those who were wounded or killed. The community members who possess greater hierarchy give a place to the perpetrator or aggressor. He remains in the community with the sole privilege of being on display for all while lying in a hammock, until they know the fate of their victim or injured person. If the victim that has been hurt dies, there are two possibilities. The first one is to hang the body of the victim from a tree in the middle of the jungle, and wait for worms to devour his body in the anticipated time. The second option would be to cremate the body of the victim in a mournful ritual. Usually, this is the custom.

What struck me the most about this story was knowing that the man that is waiting in the hammock, at all times receives indications of what the community is about to decide. If the victim is to be hanged from a tree in the jungle, it is regarded as vengeance for what happened to the offended community. Then our man that waits in the hammock would begin to expectorate worms from his mouth, not long after the deceased victim experiences the same in his lifeless body. If cremation occurs, then in the same way, at the time of the cremation, the calmly waiting warrior would commence throwing ashes from his mouth for many days, unable to resist the experience.

It means that the fate of one is linked to the other. Whatever happens to one will be the same for the other one. Thus, the warrior who is able to preserve life honors his victim and in some way, in the energetic level, everything is settled. The victim does not find peace until he is seen or acknowledged by his perpetrator or murderer.

This story, shared and transmitted by the Mage, made me think and rethink many times and become conscious on various levels. Everything truly comes to converge then. Powerful connections with each person that we think of or that still thinks of us are experienced day by day, far beyond what is physical. The biggest illusion of the human being is the belief that we are separated.

Love is a connection of thought. Hard to believe.

Each daybreak next to the Mage was the customary ritual where we brought this into our awareness. Ninety minutes before sunrise is the time when the cosmos gives us a source of inspiration to be creative. Everything awakens with such force, that we elevate what is new and reborn together with the Universe. The rocks make the most of a conversation amongst themselves and we respect that, in each one of them, we find a sage at rest. Breathing deeply, feeling that our heart is capable of smiling and, in that moment, raising a prayer to all our loved ones, the ones that still exist in this plane, the ones that have already decided to leave, and the new ones to come. The words revolve around gratitude for our body each morning, organs, cells, for the earth that sustains us, learning and appreciating the day yet to come.

The heart embraces the spirit. To live in harmony ensures the connection with the supreme, with the Universe. The body feels liberated, the daily chores stop being so heavy and we begin to know why we are back in this *round* of life. None of this is accomplished alone. All human beings, even though we don't know or may not be conscious of it, are bound in one way or another. We come to be pushed or to push others so that we all arrive. This is how I learned never to underestimate anyone who was in front of me. *La Maga and her legacy.*

To assume, therefore, the responsibility of what is done and its consequences, is a tough path, of growth. Guilt, or pretending to be distracted, in short, doesn't help much. It only brings worse consequences each day.

Anyone attempting the path of consciousness, perceives the possibility of opening the eyes to the knowledge that there is no going back nor possible blindness. Once we remove this veil, we can confront the darkest part of ourselves, and there is nothing else to do than continue with the plan that we once traced for ourselves. The mage spoke clearly,

"Life is a very serious matter and always demands a very special strength. The one who knows this and chooses this for life, also must know that there is no possible turning back. Each new step shall be more demanding, to the extent that other levels of consciousness will be revealed."

If it were a classified ad, it would read like this: "Looking for people with strength of heart; those with weakness of soul, please do not respond." Energy always chooses the pathfinder and he who remains in motion. No one can take away from another person what corresponds to them. The energy first moves within us, and then we are able to obtain it in silence, with respect. The lights we find within us are the lampposts that we find and use to avoid repeated stumbling on the assigned path.

"Welcome everyone"

Back in the old house, I walked through the halls toward my room. It was still early. My wet hair stood out in the daylight. A few people wandered through the halls and gardens of the place. However, the flowers and landscape did not need witnesses to be noticed. I abandoned myself, more calmly I began to feel the internal changes. It was difficult to find a prudent translator. I wanted silence.

From a whirlwind of thoughts to the calmness of a flowing river, I began to live in images of leaves dancing downstream. All accompanied each other; none questioned the current and its hidden force. They abandoned themselves. The surrender and the flow transmitted to the pure and vivid air. I was a little leaf and I smiled flowing down through life.

I returned to myself after floating among channels resembling new possibilities.

I had the day off and I could do what I desired. My presence before the Mage and her activities was not necessary. I felt grateful to have the space to be in quietude and freedom, after what I had experienced the previous evening with my knight.

What a transformation I had dared to live. I walked most of the morning, going through and investigating every corner around the old house, seemingly renovated before my eyes. My bare feet on the grass were a gift to the earth, which felt my gratitude. Definitely, there was a difference, or a lot of difference. It was almost noon and the sun was subtle on the landscape. I liked the weather on my face, liked feeling the heat. An idea landed between my eyebrows. I liked the notion that encircled me. I let it excite me to the point of feeling its persuasion. It had been long since I had taken myself to lunch. Determined and filled with enthusiastic decision, I went up to my room and grabbed my wallet.

Today I would invite myself for lunch.

There was a small town a few miles away and I wanted to enjoy my own company. This way I ensured I would be with myself for a short while. There was nothing more magical than to be one's own companion on the path. Today I did not want to be with people that could hasten what I still needed to perceive. Today my life was mine. I enjoyed my company; I had learned to be with myself. After a long walk on the road that led to the little town, I reflected on images that presented themselves of that which I desired. Locals looked at me strangely, sensing my tourist air. I imagined that the way I dressed called their attention. My colors accompanied me and were very vivid; they were impossible to ignore. I walked very calmly and observed each thing that I came across. Little shops along the narrow street, where everything was produced fresh daily and displayed outside, with freedom and color. The flowers continued to be the prize of the season. Observing them, I rejoiced at my internal bounty. At the end of the narrow street, immediately to the right, I saw a place where I wanted to sit with myself. A space well arranged with small tables on the outside, a place to celebrate the festivity in the presence of the sun.

I stopped at the entrance; while reading the menu, I liked the local selection and dishes. No one came to greet me. I walked to find a good table beneath the brightly colored umbrellas. I liked to look at the people walking down the street and imagine stories and tales. Women, men and children passed by without noticing my presence. Nonetheless, they all came from their parents, like me. Stories embodied in their lives were used as a daily driving force to continue. We believe that we are something out of this world, but in the end we are all the same.

The cotton tablecloth on the table was aquamarine and had been used very little. In the center was a little vase, very delicate, full of wild flowers; it delighted me by inviting me to count the petals of each one. He loves me; he loves me not; he loves me; he loves me not. Now I loved myself. Time passed in this way while I waited for the waiter and his suggestions of the day. Once again an idea came up of transforming my evening into a ritual. It was a good day for that. I felt sacred in my own company. I did not look so much outside; I stayed within me, and kept discovering the love I had for myself.

There were four chairs and I would choose one for me and another one for each of my guests today. I had decided to sit "life" at my right hand side; *I had so much to share with her*. To my left and appearing beautiful and powerful, the guest of honor, "death." I felt the gratitude that comes from her having been invited and placed in the view of my paths. On the last chair in front of me, I allowed myself to seat "love," the one that has taught me the most sacred thing. Now all was complete in my ritual.

We started a dialogue to decide what would be good to add to such a magical moment. The conversation was a main event of reality; we talked about lessons and my desire to understand the truth. Everyone moved like pieces, everyone had something to contribute. It was I who decided how and where to grow. Fear never allowed us to see life in its fragile state. In truth, life could be full of all that which was authentic and full of challenges.

Facing my fears could show me the strength of the real power of knowing myself.

Then we celebrated existence as balance. We discovered a lot in words like wisdom, faith and growth. A day like few before it, and now like many ... The hours passed by and the silence was speaking. My eyes were looking inside me when I closed them. I was alive and everyone celebrated me as I did. Maybe now that I could speak of love, I would only stay in silence, loving. Between vegetables and the aromatic water of local herbs the show had passed by. A delicious apple pie had been the crowning jewel of our day, for which I was endlessly grateful.

The mountains in the scene displayed enjoyment. The trees talked about the time that was approaching, of what could and should come for me.

I was ready to return to the house and talk with the Mage. Perhaps, being honest with myself, I would be able to have a conversation that led me to understand what I wanted from her.

Twelfth Path

"What you seek is also seeking you"

I could not find the Mage. Once back at the house, I had asked about her for almost two hours, and no one had an answer for me. Even in her physical absence I had learned that she managed to exist beyond the visible world. Not a simple thing to understand for many. Without looking at you, she looked at you. She listened to everything behind the walls from her unknown dimension. When you could find her, the first thing she asked you was exactly that which you had been hiding from. She did not give you a break. She was always there with you.

Nearly twenty-four hours had passed since my encounter with the sultan of dreams. I thought of him and what he might be doing now. I felt physically tired from everything that I had experienced. I felt odd not being able to find the Mage. This process made me feel more spiritual than ever. An awareness, complete with a silence that guided me and spoke to me. Something was happening and I dared not predict my future. *Maga*, are you there?

From the teachings I had remembered something. When the spirit somehow evolves through consciousness, the body is obliged to go through some sort of expansion, a true transformation. Consciousness expands and, as a consequence, the sacred vessel also expands. More willpower, more vitality, more responsibility. A space or container is needed that can hold all these new energies. Something told me that I had to pay for the journey I had travelled. Nothing was free; much less the processes that made us grow within. I had to be alert to what was going to be asked of me in exchange for this completed transformation.

Each time I received this type of knowledge, I had the sense that I could not control the non-tangible worlds as I pleased. Simply being there brought as a consequence the relief of my vessel. It could not be any other way.

In the wise words of the Mage's eternal expression, "what you seek is also seeking you," was found the wonderful hidden meaning: "you were looking for me when I found you."

Once again I sensed that what was learned would take me to a new dimension that I was unaware of. No surprises here. I breathed and frequently repeated to myself the remedy of the word "calm," while remaining alert. Do not do it the same way; live through it and change it. Even deeper, how frightening. The best way to reduce the symptoms of an initiation like this, was to try integrating in time with the actions that came from that which was new. We learned so that we may do something. A necessary requisite when we wanted healing was to heal ourselves.

For the sacred vessel it was not prudent to hold so much energy. After what had been learned, it was important to take a pause, so that later on we could do something with it. It was not advisable to hang onto the learning, much less plagiarize it. To heal was to act. An advertisement might say it like this: "Seeking people that practice before preaching."

I sensed my body somewhat swollen. I could notice it in my hands and feet. My rings felt tight on my fingers. A light headache and sore throat were a signal of what was imminent. My defenses were low; so many emotions in such little time had made me sick. In an instant I realized it and now it was too late. I lacked the astuteness to handle it and take a pause.

I had been carried away by a longing to grow up as I pleased. I had to withdraw to be with myself and what was coming. I was aware of this. An energetic process called disease takes us out of circulation for a while, to give the body some time to assimilate and for the soul to decide the next day's journey. With more or with less strength, it was only the next stage. I was in my bed staring out the window to the terrace. I didn't even want to think. I got into the blankets like a womb that would see me be born again. In the darkness I awaited the process that would take me to what was new. My soul and body hurt.

In bed I observed the eave of the roof that sheltered me. I felt cold and fearful. I did not want to do anything and I could not move. Everything hurt and my mind was not coordinating. At times an ancestral cry seized me. Thousands of tears flowed from my eyes without knowing why. It was a metamorphosis.

I managed to listen to the birds in the distance, the wind and the dew in the air that never ceased. The expansion of my senses could analyze and reach the unthinkable. "I am dying," was the phrase that I repeated endlessly.

Yet I dared to be strong and look at things as clearly as possible. I allowed myself to feel the process that took me to an unknown place. I listened to the ancestral hollows within me, the seashells full of ocean, incapable of becoming separate. My body was a branch of a tree that had to contort in silence in the face of the storm. The pain in my bones was unbearable, I felt them splitting in two and yet I was still whole. My soul yelled to the spirit that it should not to forget its body. I wanted to be reborn. *Maga*, are you there?

I could not see anything. Everything was very dark, confusing reality with yearning.

What was I doing here? Who was I? Why did no one know where I was? Why did I no longer need to find refuge in anyone? Never again would I use anyone to hide me from myself.

I closed my eyes and observed the same. It was my shadow that walked at night. I was wandering between the cosmos and my body. Be calm. I was brave and sought strength.

I would rather surrender. Silence.

The door suddenly opened. Faraway and in the semi-darkness I seemed to recognize the silhouette of the Mage. I felt the space come to a stop, paralyzed, and the air was very cold. Was it only my imagination, or was this really happening? She was standing still watching me and I was filling up with panic. Her silence resounded in me and I wanted to yell.

Without knowing what to do, with little strength and barely any will, I saw her and showed her my humility. I was fragile and wanted to talk, despite my lack of language. Little by little she walked toward me and got closer. She held my head with her hands; I perceived her very particular scent.

In the same quiet space, with her body language and gestures, she made me realize that I had to open my mouth to accept what she wanted me to swallow. What reached my lips and tongue was a warm liquid that started to become more and more bitter as it entered my body. As much as I tried to remove my face from such a horrible concoction, the stronger it became within me. I quieted myself and let the remedy fill my guts; immediately, I felt I should be grateful.

Even though I did not understand it, in this silence I was more comfortable; I was communicating with her without arrogance. I liked not saying anything, and at the same time, saying it all. I felt her compassion and a love that emerged from a place that I didn't know of. Slowly, I removed all my clothes till I was naked. I felt taken care of, protected and loved. With strength, she rubbed my body, each part of it, with some kind of ointment. Her hands, touching me, were those of a healer. Will she heal me or will I heal myself? *Maga* ...

In a moment, I began to feel hundreds of tiny needles passing completely through me. Very conscious, I was aware that I should not fight this dimension that seemed like pain. However, I was dizzy and had trouble breathing.

I was in her hands and had to trust. It was in this moment that I needed to trust. I did not understand the space I was in. I felt transformed to a degree where it seemed like everything was too narrow. Could it be I was outside of my body, or that perhaps I was dead? I breathed, calmed down, and trusted.

After having covered me with the ointment, she wrapped me with newspaper. I must have had a lot of fever, since my lips were burning and the tremors left me with no strength.

It was a strange sensation to see myself covered in newspaper. Yet, this unlikely insanity began to be a relief. The fever and humidity were trying to leave my body. Could the Mage cure the heart?

Maybe she was already inside, working on it for a long time. She placed my clothes on top of the newspaper, with great calmness. Throughout the difficulty of defining what was happening, and the pain of my process, I think I felt her lips on my forehead. I was able to cry and breathe. It hurts feeling love. This was a love I didn't know of. Maternal, supreme and magnificent. I could not explain it; it was a matter of living it.

Suddenly silence was broken and his voice came from the light. I tried to listen to something; it was difficult to pay attention because I was stunned. I stayed attentive. He spoke in murmurs. I was able to hear some things. It seemed like someone religious or a monk in meditation, who, at times, let some phrases escape that were almost imperceptible to catch.

"Don't fight," he said. "I am here to talk with all of your being in all of its planes," he continued. "Your body is on its way to know its own spirit, try to be honest with yourself as soon as possible. Do not betray yourself more. The past only helps you to continue on the journey if you have learnt the lesson. Do not be afraid, only travel forever and ever. Walk."

I didn't know anything more; I must have passed out or lost my mind. I remembered with attention the few words that I was able to hear.

The fever continued and I didn't know any more if what I had experienced was real or a dream.

I was confused.

When I opened my eyes she was not there, or perhaps had never been there.

Who gave me the remedy?

Who swaddled me in messages?

I remembered again what I had heard from her, or from me, and the shivers returned, almost to the point of convulsions.

To make love with someone breaks with the souls of the others that came before. Let your body fill with life; make existence convene its perpetuity. Hiding behind your skin will not help you; the one who does not thank its body and does not gratify its infinite journey gets lost. The Universe can be spent giving you opportunities. Look at yourself with dignity. When the time comes to open the heart, you will gain full freedom to spread your wings.

I saw her in the distance one more time; I was cautious to believe in the unreality of the moment. It was my own yearning to know it was her. My desire made it so that her shadow was intertwined with mine.

"Nothing to do, everything is done"

The lights of the dawn dared to stir me up little by little.
I vaguely recall that I woke up in the midst of a deep silence.
Everything looked in order in my room.
Nothing strange was happening.
I sat up gradually. I was still dizzy and nauseous.

I began to perceive that my senses were different... I observed with more brilliance; I perceived the scent and feeling of the sheets; I was able to sense the wind that was waking with the morning.

My heart was bursting with love, sighing and breathing, grateful and nearly dancing with me. The experience of feeling a love that I had never noticed before was something to behold; what an experience I was living. My body, still soaked in sweat, distilled sacred water; this is how I experienced it...

When I became aware of my sacred vessel, I realized that it was still wrapped in newspaper. I started to remove it little by little. As I observed the date printed on the newspaper, with images and a language that was foreign to me, I said to myself, "old news."

Everything stays behind.

I was very thirsty; I was hungry and I was alive. I recalled the trance I had been in. I couldn't compare the experience that I had gone through with anything similar, even the journey with which the sacred plants had once gifted me.

My mind dared to appear. Subtly I questioned myself in a different way.

I noticed that the new foundations would break the preconceptions of things to come.

I would have to watch over me. Feeling certain in my purpose was the most important mission, and I already had one of the greatest signs in knowing myself as the owner of my life. It was a matter of observing patiently. "The changes are always wonderful opportunities," I repeated to myself endlessly.

Enthusiastic, happy and grateful, I took off what I was wearing. Completely naked, I prepared to go out to the terrace. I continually thanked my humble abode that had been witness to my desire to grow and to heal. In the distance I noticed the clothesline near the house. Tablecloths and white sheets allowed themselves to be heard, like the nourishing applause of the wind. I observed the faint glow of the last stars and planets that were opposed to being concealed by the daylight. I was able to smile and my soul felt a very unique joy.

I accepted the gift with amazement, when I noticed that sounds were more defined.

New echoes mixed with old ones made the perfect symphony. More alert, I observed the process of having awakened to a new dimension. Each dewdrop was sliding into my soul. I started to savor the aroma of the trees that witnessed me. My body, in unison with the earth, allowed me to see my own essence.

I observed the cosmos dawning slowly. The greatness of the constellations enveloped me. Everything was spinning and now I was spinning with the whole. I was being born again and I did not negate the expansion and the scope.

Maga, are you there?

The contentment left me exposed; I wanted to burst into laughter without knowing why. I liked listening to myself.

The wise stones were damp and the small crickets were hiding, shy at my happiness.

I was not the same. I would let others discover me when they were able to see themselves in me.

I felt that I had gone within a path filled with silence and little explanation. I didn't need to know about love, much less seek it, beg for it, or suffer it.

"I am all there is, beyond words." I felt light in my arms, which ended in wings.

Eyes like beacons that guided from within. I listened to the ocean waves and, one by one, they crashed into my firmly planted feet.

I felt the expansion. I was fused with the Universe.

I made a trip in seconds by closing my eyes and feeling that I was in my mother's womb. It appeared as though I was looking at stars and everything that shapes the vast Universe.

I had the sensation of being held and seeing the sky as if it was covering the most sacred thing that I have, the earth that I walked on.

To sense the familiarity of that sky and compare it to the sensation of being inside of my mother, was the gift.

The time to descend and continue on had arrived. Time had been fair and kind with me.

I wanted to run and seek the Mage, hug her and tell her in silence that everything was in order, the lesson had been learned. I rushed into my room and dressed with what I was able to find. The only thing that mattered was to go upstairs and find the Mage.

Before knocking on her door, I stopped. I paused. I felt an enormous respect toward her. Her space and dwelling should be held sacred.

I recapitulated in my mind what I should say. I was restless and happy. I wanted to share all my experience with her.

I knocked on her door several times, but it did not open. Nothing was happening. However, I could hear noises inside the bedroom and I could see the light of a lamp that had been left on despite the daylight. *Maga* ...

I waited for a period of time that I considered prudent. Then I decided to take a stroll near the forest that surrounded the ancient house.

Maga, my *Maga* ... Where have you gone? Did you leave? Are you here? *Maga*? I walked and walked. *Maga*.

I waited for father Sun to appear completely. Under my feet I could feel the sounds of drums within the earth.

The celebration of my ancestors and a sacred force that accompanied me were making the day begin like an extraordinary party. *Maga* ...

Along the road, after a long time walking, I picked up all the feathers of the birds that were gifts in the form of signals. I thought I should keep them and start to build my own wings for the day when it was my turn to fly. I wanted to have a large pair of wings, well constructed of paths and signals, in order to have a safe flight.

I knew now that I could not stop. More paths would bring more feathers and this would be an eternal and safe flight.

I returned to the ancient house, my path for the past days. Upon entering the usual hall adjoining with the breakfast area, I noticed the strange look that everyone was giving me.

I didn't understand what was happening and it felt uncomfortable holding that much energy.

For a moment I even thought that I was still naked and that was what provoked their curiosity and alarm.

I cautiously checked my attire, in case that was the reason. Almost always we are concealed.

I smiled to myself.

In my silent thoughts and in front of so many strange gazes, I said to myself, "What can the others understand about the processes that each one of us must experience? Nothing, certainly nothing."

So silence began to be my best ritual to leave others with their own answers.

I sat on the sofa where I could savor my morning coffee once again. To the extent that people started to parade around me, I felt joy in being able only to observe. I enjoyed the way that they also observed me with respect and gratitude for my existence that morning.

I finished the coffee and I was grateful for the space that they gave me by not questioning or meddling with me. The silence I was harboring now was allowing a conversation with myself that I had to attend to.

I felt less of that need to fight or feel anguish to continue searching outside of myself.

Everything was complete and belonged to diversity. I was feeling finally at home. There was no other place more beautiful than this dwelling inside of me.

My piece of property was flourishing like magic and I wanted to welcome everyone. I was loving myself for being able to love.

I rested some time alone in my room after the walk and the coffee. I needed some tranquil space more than anything else.

There it was easier for me to generate conscious life. I didn't think so much of the Mage. Everything was transforming second by second.

I got ready to pack knowing that the time had come to conclude everything that I had started.

There was still work to do during the day and I was aware that I would be next to the Mage to share that which was the most sacred about her: her presence. To discover her as something new was a challenge.

I carefully examined my luggage and its contents. While I was packing, I realized how strange it felt to look at my dresses. The sensation that was calling my attention was a feeling that they were not mine. They seemed like borrowed clothing. I asked myself where I had been when I decided to buy so many things that were now not nearly close to even the shadow of my light.

I had to laugh at myself. I made the decision to keep the most basic things. I wanted light and authentic luggage. Something that would allow me to live with life.

I thought of the knight and his armor, of the tattoo on my soul, family, my children.

Time stopped in other ways. Companions of destinies, travelers of the same paths, over and over again in many lives and sequences.

All that was missing was seeing the Mage and maintaining silence in her presence and her path.

Beautiful woman, filled with wisdom, patience and paths.

The experience of each instant makes you heroic and nobody should or could take that which you have lived.

Kind of heart, you open up to teach that which is sweet and that which is salty of a life with dignity, to whoever wants it.

She counts on new experiences, be they good or not so good ones. "There are no bad days, only days of growth." The healer of souls, that is your name, filled with powerful plants possessing seeds that open the soul, you accompany the sowing because you know about the earth and its dimension. Looking now at the stars, feel the cold that is capable of transporting you to warmth.

Trust in your steps, perceive the paths that you must crystallize. The time has come. It is time to close in order to open. Conclude the work we started in order to continue the commitment that we must continue.

I was ready to go down, with my luggage much lighter. "My office should now be the path."

I liked to listen to the sound of the necklaces that I was wearing. I felt that I took each step with gratitude. The time had come to transcribe the Universe. Knowledge by the handful to the one that wants the magic.

A door opened and I gave thanks to God. There was a sacred silence. They awaited my arrival with enthusiasm.

The Earth was pleased at seeing herself protected by rituals of gratitude.

La Maga appeared.
La Maga was celebrated by her own magic.
La Maga had arrived.
La Maga that I am now.

I want to whisper in your ear and perhaps
you will be able to hear me.
Everything is always conceived in perfect
sequences; a dot here, a space there.
Connect the dots and trace the inexplicable,
translate the language that speaks in silence.
The stories are born, grown, reproduced
and transformed, they never die.
The pages that follow are the path for you.

Maga, are you there?

www.earthedition.org